PRETEND
WE'VE NEVER MET

PRETEND
WE'VE NEVER MET

JONIS AGEE

PEREGRINE SMITH BOOKS

SALT LAKE CITY

First Edition

93 92 91 90 89   5 4 3 2 1

Copyright © Jonis Agee

This is a Peregrine Smith Book, published by Gibbs Smith, Publisher, P.O. Box 667, Layton, Utah 84041

Design by J. Scott Knudsen

Cover illustration by Scott Snow

Printed and bound in the United States of America.

LIBRARY OF CONGRESS CATALOGING-IN-PUBLICATION DATA
Agee, Jonis.
    Pretend we've never met / Jonis Agee.
       p. cm.
    ISBN 0-87905-134-5 : (pbk)
    I. Title
    PS3551.G4P7   1989
    813'.54—dc19   88.39568
                             CIP

The paper used in this publication meets the minimum requirements of American National Standard for Information Sciences—Permanence of paper for Printed Library Materials, ANSI Z39.48–1984 ∞

*For Paul McDonough and
Brenda Bobbitt*

Acknowledgments

The author wishes to thank the National Endowment for the Arts for its fellowship and support of this work.

Thanks for Lon Otto for his advice, patience, and friendship while these stories grew.

Stories have previously appeared in the following publications:

"Mercury" appeared in *Glitch* and also was published as a chapbook by Toothpaste Press.

"The Man of Sorrows" appeared in *Glitch* and was published as a chapbook by Fodder Editions.

"Stiller's Pond" appeared in *Mpls-St. Paul* and in *Stiller's Pond,* an anthology by New Rivers Press.

"Today" appeared in *Phoebe.*

"What She Knew" appeared in *Gallimaufry.*

"The Dead of July" appeared in *Vinyl.*

"After the Movies" appeared in *Vinyl.*

"Young" appeared in *Sing, Heavenly Muse!* and *Gallimaufry.*

"The Geographers" appeared in *Truck.*

"What the Fall Brings" appeared in *Story Quarterly.*

"At Last" appeared in *Hawk-Wind.*

"Farm Story" appeared in *Moons and Lion Tailes* and *Sailing the Road Clear.*

Contents

Mercury

At first it had gone relatively unnoticed, or perhaps they had done very little then—prying the letter *R* off—maybe the initial of one of the neighborhood kids, or just the loosest chrome on the car, an elegantly printed name, MERCURY, spread decorously across the wide wide front end, still intact after eleven years. Around the same time they had crushed some sort of fruit on one chrome bumper, it could have been thrown, it dried in orange pulpy strands like a larger species of some South American insect. Of course, the usual fingerprints and odd smearings left on the hood and trunk. They were never *seen,* these children, but their mark was always visible in some minor way. What could he expect—leaving it out in the alley behind his small house and yard. It was too large to fit in the single-car garage. He had forced it a couple of times, but had scraped the right side good in a long, even slice. No way to completely shut the garage door then. It always came to rest on the bumper, so what was the point?

There was no hiding the fact of its existence. There it was: long and wide and square. He had never even pushed the gas pedal to the floor, there was no need—it hunched at stoplights waiting to spring out.

He had to hold the power brake tightly then—a light tap on the gas and off he went—rocking around corners, floating down highways. A car much too big for a single person, he knew, and much too expensive to run, he knew.

Ten years ago he had marveled at such cars, sleek and luxurious, yet assertive in their taut linear design. Always present. Not a laughable VW toy or something modest, middle of the road, like a Chevy. It was consciously extravagant—a relic now of that time. There was no economy in that 390-horsepower engine, the six-way power seat that still worked. Who needed the embarrassing suggestiveness of reclining seats? Here was the vehicle as hotel, each seat comfortably taking the length, it seemed, of a human body.

At night in early fall, when he had first gotten the car, he would lie on the front seat, radio turned low to the back channels—no FM then, but not necessary either. It seemed right that this beauty should only have AM on its three-position sound system, good as the day it was built. FM had been phony symphonies, things a Parklane owner wouldn't be interested in. Then the neighbor kids were in bed, families settled in for the night, dogs taken indoors from the small fenced yards, and an odor of evening cooking still lingering in the air, mingled with the smell of dried leaves and drying grass. The metallic scent of hot summer gone. A light breeze brushing through the car once in a while. He was happy.

But now, something was happening. First the *R* had disappeared. He regretted it, but promised himself that someday he would go to a junkyard and get another or maybe even put an ad in one of those old car magazines.

Then they began to throw things at it: in the fall a rotting apple or two, but now he discovered small dents weekly, and another letter had disappeared—the *Y*—one of his favorites, spread wide with modern yet classical grace. He had been particularly pleased with it. He tried to think of the last names of all his neighbors—maybe that would be a clue. He even considered going to the city directory and checking the adjoining blocks, but he never did. By the time they had taken the *U,* he had given up on ever replacing the hood letters.

But it continued. He still imagined it was children, who would stop at the letters and rocks. He began again to try to put the car in the garage, but its rear end remained visible and vulnerable. How could their parents let them out at night? In addition, he caught one bumper against the metal garage door frame, and the car pulled the garage frame askew. The door no longer returned properly. His bumper, that lovely chrome expanse, had been pulled slightly off so that now it hung lower on one side, but not by much. Fortunately, it was again the right side, so he didn't have to look at it much. The Mercury was still in remarkable shape. No point to lament a few dents or scratches.

But it continued. Every morning, all summer, he woke to the fury of their small hands. Why did they pick on his car? Why not the neighbors' small sporty compacts—noses buried in the lilac bushes behind their garages? Was it because his car sat there, encroaching openly on their territory? Other cars did have to drive slowly, carefully around it, edging inches away from its pale, metallic-green sides.

In addition to the front letters, someone had diligently removed—he didn't know how—the Parklane plate on the left side. Now he had to face the empty holes and darker, unfaded paint beneath it each day. It had been an excellent design: neat, sharp, no-nonsense letters framed in a field of red reflector-speckled paint. He couldn't understand their obsession with the names, and words on his car. Why not rip off the aerial or slash the tires or smash the windows, why this slow and painful dismemberment, as if denaming it were in a way disarming its power? What next?

It remained. He still drove it. Of course, their constant attack was beginning to tell now. The paint, once nearly flawless and certainly extraordinary on a car this old, was dented and nicked, fading and darkening in spots. He couldn't imagine why small flecks of rust began to appear. A larger dent in the right rear end, where they had thrown something the shape of a field stone against the car, began to rust out. At first the old paint had cracked but clung, then finally it had fallen in the summer heat and rain. He had promised himself that he would go to the Mercury dealer nearby, purchase the paint, and at least repaint the spot. But now it was too late for that.

At that time the Mercury lay like a boat shivering in rough waters each night, and he awoke each morning to new storm damage. They seemed intent on prying off, unbolting, unscrewing, breaking (but only at last resort) each and every detachable or chrome item on the car. He knew they were working on the bumpers. He pledged he would stay up on guard all night to catch them at it; but he didn't. As if some agreement had tacitly grown up between them, he continued to love and grieve over his car; but he also continued to sacrifice it, unwilling to protect it. As if it had a hard lesson coming from the world, like a mother sending her sons off to the war, certain they would be wounded or killed, but certain it was necessary and right, he could not, would not, move the car. Yes, he had thought of renting garage space, looked up a few numbers in the Sunday papers, had never, though, gotten around to calling.

When they were nearly finished with the outside, and it had taken them a while, several weeks to get the bumpers (he had had to take sleeping pills a few nights to get through the racket of their work in the alley), he began to leave the Mercury unlocked. Whereas the car had earlier seemed haughty in its grandeur, with an old-world embellished flavor, now it seemed proud in its new naked aspect, less imposing but more moving in its tragic, ridiculous appearance. A car meant to be decorated, to be fawned over, now like a general without medals and ribbons. The artistic chrome moldings were gone from the sides, as were wire grills, big plated hubcaps, side mirrors adjustable with levers from the *inside* (a feature just then appearing on the new cars). They had even managed to remove the little levers themselves from their slots, and the metal frames of the slots—everything, in fact.

By fall he could only drive the car during the day because the headlights and taillights had been neatly extracted: lenses, bulbs, glass covers, chrome holders, the works—even his wiring. At times he marvelled at their thoroughness. Wondered, too, where the hell the stuff was going. Should he discreetly check the neighborhood garages? What if he came upon one of the six-foot bumpers shining there in the darkness—what would he do? No, he'd best leave it alone.

Then, too, he speculated about the workers. They couldn't be the kids he saw around the neighborhood during the day; those were just children, eight, ten years old. No. It seemed to be more carefully orchestrated work than fifteen- or sixteen-year-olds could manage, this dismantling of the car—as if hands that yearly took down the Christmas tree now set to work, maybe in a tired but patient fashion, to remove the car from itself. Yes, it looked like adult work. Not malicious at all. This thought comforted him.

In October he again lay out in the car at night in the alley, listening to the radio, local music stations, occasionally a signal from further out—Nebraska or Canada—but mostly just local DJs. Request night songs, girls to boys, all traveling in their imaginary cars out of their houses and down the streets with the music to sail them along, happy and excited by the songs they gave each other. He was glad for them, smiling as he lay on his back, arms crossed over his chest, feet crossed and propped on the window sill of the car. Occasionally he would play with one of the three switches for the power seat, adjusting to an inch higher or lower, tilting back or up, the middle of the seat rotating slightly, like a human pelvis. The disc jockeys pleased, him too. Their patter had remained the same over the years: a little bawdier, more explicit perhaps, like the music, but still fast and clever, full of incredible energy, even late at night. And a sameness he enjoyed, a continuity, nothing really new to get used to, to jar him into a different place, the same songs over and over, introduced by a thousand inventions, he enjoyed it all. On those clear October nights in his car (he really didn't need to drive at night, after all, the pleasure was still there, just to be in it, folded resting in its comfort and weight, it was more *there* than anything he had ever known, he felt), he could see the stars if he looked out the window. He could smell the world. He could know it all.

And then in November, when it was too cold to spend his evenings out there, they began to work on the inside. The outside of the car was now the stripped shell he often saw in pictures of assembly lines in automobile factories— the busy men with torches and wrenches, just on the verge of applying all the superficial aspects of the car. He saw it in that light now. He realized that it was something he had not known before, what was really there. The car seemed then more compact, more self-centered than ever, yet also larger and more sprawling. It seemed to take up more room. He marveled at its growth, at its new potential and stature. It appeared to be growing younger, but hadn't assumed the uncertainty of youth. It was stronger.

Of course, he could no longer drive the Mercury, though they considerately left the license plates on—see, they weren't irresponsible teenagers, he argued. They had taken the windows though, first the side ones, not so bad, but cold. Then when the door handles and gear shift and pedals had been stripped, they somehow removed the windshield. They hadn't broken it, he knew, no glass littering the ground around the car. Next, all the dash dials. He didn't regret the clock, the one thing that has never worked in the car, it stopped and started by some mysterious process of its own. He rather missed the oil, gas and temperature dials though, little round agents metering his performance. He liked to watch their red arrows jump up when he started the car, which, of course, he couldn't do now. The steering wheel was gone by late November. He continued to be amazed by their efficiency, they took *everything*. Still the car persisted, without brakes, ashtrays, dials, overhead dome light, glove compartment, armrests, lighters, flow-through ventilators, the works. He never looked under the hood these days, but assumed that the engine would be intact until the interior was finished.

His one moment of regret, to be expected, was the morning he noticed that the radio was gone. They had done it neatly, humanely, he realized. No dangling wires, thick black cords, truncating sounds, missing connections remained behind. No. There was simply a hole. A neat incision. There was nothing to see. He felt that finally the car had been gutted like an animal. He was certain that the parts were carefully husbanded for later use. Nothing left, but still it bothered him. He could see that this was the end of something now. Again he considered putting a stop to it—but how? He probably couldn't. Where would he start? What if he recovered the radio—even the other parts which surely lurked in the neighboring garages and basements—what then? The mystery of the car would never be disclosed to him. He could hardly put it back together. No, this process, which had suddenly, abruptly reached a painful place for him—and it was *real* pain now, he knew that, and *real* longing, he knew that too, no, this process could not stop now. Maybe they had waited that long for the radio because they knew, somehow, what it would mean to him, the crisis and pain. Maybe they had tried to hold it off, as he must have, too. And maybe they had his point of view, that the *radio* was the *center* of the car.

When they took the six-way power seat control and later the front seat itself, he felt resignation tinged with sadness, not despair actually. In fact, it was also relief, he thought. Now it was over. As if he had held his breath for a long time, maybe since the radio had gone, now it was really over. He thought he wouldn't care anymore, tried to convince himself that since he couldn't sit in the damn thing, why bother caring about it. But he couldn't stop himself, it turned out, from visiting what was the essence of the car—a heavy steel frame enclosed with panels of sheet metal. They were working on the insulation and padding these days, like insects picking flesh from a carcass; there was nothing wasted. The doors and trunk were soon gone, too.

In mid-December the snow began, often drifting high against the backyard fence and the car parked right outside it. There was no question of protecting it now. He noticed that the engine was gone during a thaw after Christmas. Once in a while he sighted the car from his back windows, its color gone now, too, as if the paint had been carefully cleansed. A light coat of rust covered the car body. Finally, he couldn't see the car. It was a terrible winter, more blizzards then anyone—even older farmers who should know better than the rest—could remember. He quit using his back door; the snow drifted it shut. He now concentrated on the front of the house, spending hours digging himself out each day. It took all his energy; he forgot about the car in back. For days, weeks, it didn't exist, until something would remind him of it: a letter *R* in a form similar to the perfect row which once crossed the front end, or the glint of chrome on his toaster—the peculiar distortion of his face in its mirror would remind him of the magnificent bumpers or hub-caps. He couldn't stand anything the color of pale green now. It brought a fit of remorse which was only dispelled by much snow shoveling.

Generally, however, he forgot about the car. If it existed, it was his memory of it only—the length and luxury of its body, the crafting of the details, the ultimate thoughtfulness of its design. He didn't recall its destruction—neither the early random violence against it, nor the later careful execution.

When spring finally came, late and long-awaited with the great piles of snow melting into liquid ground, he was once again able to use the back door. On the first day of his return to the alley, he was not surprised to see that the Mercury was gone. He had forgotten about it entirely over the past month, and now there was nothing to insure its memory—not a bolt, not a shred of glass or metal, not even grooves where the weight of its bulk had settled into the ground. It was gone. He was certain it had been there once, but it was clearly not there now. It seemed better that way.

Stiller's Pond

Look, I just want to tell
you what it's like out there, what the wind and the river
do. How still. How I am walking by the pond in Stiller's
cow pasture. It was January, like now, and twenty below
zero, before the light comes up. I can't sleep. I want to
be somewhere.

The pond is frozen into these little waves the wind
puts there, starched on the top. The kids won't be skating there anyway, not since a long time ago. The pond
doesn't have to freeze sheet clean, because none of us
would ever be skating there again. As if it knew, the pond
always froze in peculiar shapes, as if someone was still
under there trying to get out.

If you stood over those places where the water bobbed
dark, speckled with stuff churning up from the bottom,
you'd think you could see a face pressed and distorted
against that little skim of ice, like something from dinner
your mom put plastic over and plopped in the fridge, until
later when you looked, it was unfamiliar again through
the moisture-beaded wrap. At one end the cattails stood
at attention, still as boys in ROTC, backs swayed in a pose
you knew they'd never be able to walk out of, and little

tatters of dried leaves waved like flags from the stalks. Around them lay the litter of last summer.

It was in those left, standing the way they are now, that they found her, hair tangled around. They had to chop part of it off to get her out. That's what the adults told us, and if that quick thaw hadn't come up, it would've been April before she was noticed. He was a different matter, bobbing like a cork in the hole that stayed over the spring. Still, it was hard to tell the difference between him and the water at a distance; you couldn't really get very close. But the thaw sent him skimming over the edge so that his tuber-white face rose up like a signal at sea, and someone finally saw it. I suppose it was lucky that the thaw came—and the kids. Though they knew they wouldn't be skating with the ice that way, they came down to the pond as always, just to fool around. Throw rocks. Build a fire. They weren't permitted to build fires anywhere else. But somehow, it was okay if you had a legitimate winter excuse like skating. Sledding was marginal, but skating was okay for fire building. Being kids, they figured the permission was for location rather than activity, so they went to Stiller's pond whenever the arson rose up in their hearts.

To this day, I can't look at those cattails without thinking of the way they told the little ones to pull the dried leaves and stalks for kindling—and the confusion they must have felt when the lady's hair wouldn't let go of them. She was face up, too, like she was sleeping in bed at home, watching the stars through her little attic window before nodding off. She'd seen a lot more since then, every night anchored there like a boat, her arms treading water gently like oars holding her steady. And the hard part was when they finally dragged her in, men in hip boots with hay hooks and ropes so they could get a grip on her, her eyes plucked out by the turtles, removed with the skill of surgeons so the lids fell gracefully, sunken over the holes.

Surprised they had left the rest of her, the men said, knowing the winter hunger of turtles drifting sleepily to the surface for oxygen before they dropped back like stones to the bottom mud. And strange, how the water had filled in the scars on her face, softened the bones until she became sweet and round and beautiful to the men, who recognized her only from the long blond hair—the dirt rinsed from it by the month in the water—and from the broken front teeth. And I think that was what bothered them the most—that she came out of the water better than she went in, that they were able to see her firsthand the way he must have, in his heart, when he would meet her at Stiller's pond after her parents were long asleep, and after her sisters and brothers were long asleep, and after the cows were long settled and the pigs and the horses heavy in sleep from their day's work, even the poultry sleeping on one leg in the roosts, as passive as camels in the dark stench of the henhouse.

And old man Stiller, refusing to help pull her out, refusing the use of his team, his wagon, his ropes, refusing the use of his blankets to wrap her in, and finally refusing her body in his house, even in his barn, where she might have lain like an animal in a stall until the fires softened the ground enough to dig even a shallow hole for her. And the mother, as hard as the father, and the children staring out the windows like portholes at the distant ocean of events they couldn't begin to understand. Incurious as the buildings that held them, they never asked, even later, for the grave of their sister. And only the fact that the children weren't allowed to come again to the pond to skate or build their fires ever served notice to them that their sister had floated like a log for a month in their cow pond, had been dragged out like a burlap bag of drowned cats behind Rofer's buggy horse and been wrapped in his wife's quilt, never to be used again, and stayed wrapped like that until put in a homemade box with the dull nickel nails winking out of the mismatched corners, and been dropped with a clattering bang into the shallow hole of frozen dirt and covered once more into darkness, only to resurface in May, when the ground heaved her up again, like the pond before it, as if something in her must have the light of day, the light of night, and been buried once more, a final time, with huge stones placed on the coffin to hold it down the nine feet they had dug to be certain that this time the body, holding its quilt around it like a cape, would not wriggle its way back into their lives.

Grandmother told the children that she was coming back for her eyes. Parents told the children to ignore what Granny said, she was just trying to scare them. But they told the children never to skate on Stiller's pond again, never. And the one time they tried—and each of them did—they got whipped, hard enough to make an impression. So when they became our parents, they told us never to go to Stiller's pond, as it was still called, and we got whipped hard enough to make the same impression. At least we never skated there. That was as specific as they had made it, and we were specific in our obedience. What we did was spend summer afternoons there, hooking turtles and dragging them up on shore, turning them over with sticks, because some of them were snappers and we couldn't tell which, so they all got treated to our punishment—beaten and prodded with sticks the big ones could snap in two. We would watch, thrilled at the sight of the pointed beak, which we knew had plucked an eyeball out of its socket with the ease of pulling a grape from the arbor vines. Though some insisted their parents had told them to look on the bellies of the old turtles to find which ones had taken her eyes because we would find their image there still, we never found such a thing and soon enough stopped believing we would discover a transparent hole where she could look out, still trying to see things she shouldn't. But for a while it had worked, and

I remember our fear when we turned each turtle over onto
its back, the claws waving helplessly in the paddling feet
as we took turns checking the underside. The younger
children, overcome, would go screaming and crashing
through the cattails and weeds up the banks until we told
them it was all right.

The Stiller children moved away, died, fought in wars
and came home. Always someone survived to work the
farm, though in the community heart, they were stained
with this memory. They followed a pattern, too, the old
ones would hint, only to be shushed by the parents. The
darker gleam of interest would lead us aside one time,
finally when we were old enough, and the rest of the story
would follow. How when they dragged the man out,
unlike the Stiller girl, he had been eaten at, like a piece
of suet hung on a tree for birds. There were peck marks
all over the front of his face and body, the clothes ripped
to threads on the front, intact on the back. This what they
discovered when they rolled him over. The whiteness that
had revealed him was the remaining uneaten chunk of
cheek and the milk white bone, polished by the silky bodies of small fish swimming in and out of the face. The men,
in particular, couldn't stand this story, because *everything,*
the old women would insist and look long and hard at
the boys, *everything* was chewed on. And when they were
finished with that, the turtles turned him over and gnawed
the rest.

That was bad enough, but the worst part was that no
one could identify him. Stiller wouldn't come near him,
and rumors had it that both the hired man and the oldest
boy had disappeared that night. Mrs. Stiller never spoke
a word about it. She might have identified the rags left
on the body at least, but no—so he was buried in another
shallow grave next to the girl's, only he didn't come up
in the spring. In fact, by the time they began digging the
hole to proper depth in May, the box had sunk another

two feet and filled with water. When they tried to move it, the seams burst and the thing fell apart in their hands. Inside there was even less of the man than before. Almost a skeleton, the men told people. As if he couldn't wait. That was handy though, because when they made a new box, they could make it half the regular size, just dump the bones in, and save a lot of work digging the deeper hole, too.

As I'm walking out here by Stiller's pond, I remember the old mystery and fear that always mingled in the air around the place. Now, of course, I understand that it was not knowing—the obscenity of the two missing men—that made it impossible for our parents and grandparents to tell us the truth, and therefore, to let us continue at Stiller's pond. The other man was never heard from again, whichever he was. Maybe he was at the bottom of Stiller's pond, weighted with the heavy sleeping bodies of turtles. During the summer, the cows still walk in their ritual paths to the pond, still muddy the edges, plowing the ground with their hooves, leaving pocks that freeze in uneven holes to trip small feet in winter. The cattails still grow at that one end, waving graceful and lithe as women. Sometimes I almost imagine I see the hair they chopped off so many years ago to pull her out, still woven like a basket to trap the silvery fish that lurk in the cool, dark shallows we can't quite reach when we hunt here as children. And out in the middle there's the tree limb that broke off long ago, and then the tree itself dropped to the ground and was sawed up and hauled away, leaving only the limb humped up like a sea serpent, dark and sinewy, along whose length ride the turtles that rise like ancient people from ancient sleep every spring and crawl up the back of the limb to sun, their necks stretching the tenderness where the skin is paper-thin and throbbing with a heart that once fed on the eyes of a women who tried to cross the pond one winter.

As I start across the pond under the sliver of moon that lies like a knife in the night sky, I remember the last thing our grandmothers told us, the last whispered secret that leaked out of those lips withered by year after year of disappointment and concealment: They weren't wearing skates. And that's why, they always declared with malicious joy, you can't go there—ever, you hear—ever. Thus sealing forever in our hearts the desire for the place, a desire that can never be satisfied, a desire we give to our children for Stiller's pond.

CybeLee's Life Story

When she was fourteen, CybeLee watched a man sink into the sudden clay pit of street they were repairing outside her house. Her parents didn't want her too close to the men, so she simply watched, out of their range, from her upstairs window. Thus it was that she had a unique bird's-eye view as his head sank into the soupy mixture, never to reappear again. After that, whenever she made ham hocks and noodles, she thought about him, the way the pink knuckle of flesh turned over and over in the boiling water.

Once CybeLee told her friends she was going on a trip and checked into the local motel for two days. She called room service for food. She drank wine she had brought with her hidden like heavy books in the corners of her suitcase. But that's not the point of this story. Nor is it the way she walked around in nothing but her underwear, knowing that the windows were open but the distance too great across the wide face of city for anyone to pick her out in particular. What satisfied her was watching the movie at 7 A.M. on HBO, the sound turned up enough to blot out the departing families in similar rooms around her, and later crouching in the tub like an animal waiting for the noise of the maid's cart outside the door to leave.

It had rained all week when CybeLee went down to the basement again to check on the laundry. First she stepped into the small stream coming from the dug-out part where she never swept or walked. Then she followed it carefully, allowing it to obliterate her footsteps. The pile of towels she had left by the washer were soaked, resistant to her foot when she nudged them. And when she lifted the pile, its weight made her stagger. The outline remained on the floor all day, like the smear of an animal struck by a car, and all day she ran the same load over and over, satisfied only when the towels began to unravel in a thinning of cloth.

But she wasn't alone. CybeLee had plenty of admirers, friends, people who called her up on the phone and asked questions. "Do you take the newspaper?" She tried not to be rude, only placing the receiver back in a courtesy of silence, not wanting to call attention to their mistake. With others it was different. Admirers seemed to feed on her indifference, which was unintentional. She would get up to make a cup of tea as they talked earnestly of their plans. She would forget to come back, and be discovered repotting geraniums on the back porch. They accepted her dirt-tinged embrace with gratitude. And friends, well CybeLee was the best of friends with many people. Everyone assumed she was their only friend and only occasionally was the jealousy flare-up like dogs in strange neighborhoods. Mostly everyone kept to their own yards and waited for her to walk by, call up. Those who wrote letters were soon forgotten altogether though. Getting a letter only confused CybeLee, and by the time she should have answered it, she'd already had enough conversation with the person in her mind. Feeling satisfied, she never actually wrote back. Sometimes she waited to open the letters until she could sense what was inside. No point in being surprised. CybeLee was afraid of surprises. Even the good ones with presents always seemed, in retrospect, to be tinged with disappointment. Only the bad ones seemed just what they should be.

It would be nice to think you were crazy, CybeLee decided. Then you wouldn't know that confusion of the erroneous appearance of sun on a cloudy day. Though she had, for a time, tried to be crazy, actually crazy, walking in front of cars crazy, CybeLee had always failed. Now she was stuck with her senses pinching at her like new shoes and her memories sucking her down the pipe like bathwater. Curiosity dragged her along like a willful dog on a leash. It was a relief to fall asleep in front of the TV like a middle-aged man in a Barcalounger, his stomach pillowing a tilted beer can.

CybeLee thought she never apologized, but she always did. How could there be this discrepancy, you ask? She's not crazy; she does her laundry. Here's a hint: inside of churches and libraries she got the same sick churning in her intestine. When she read about disasters in the newspaper, earthquakes, fires, murders, she always asked, did I do that? She intended to help, and did nothing, leaning back in the oak chair until she felt the joints loosen.

Once she'd found the neighbor's cat cringing in a manger of hay across the road in her rented barn. When she picked it up, the hind leg dangled in half, the skin pulled up like a skirt to the hip, leaving the ragged white bone broken apart like a soda cracker. Replacing it in the bloody hay, she had gone back across the road into her house and locked the door. Always after that, when she saw a cat trotting along prettily, she imagined the hind leg a grate of bone on the concrete.

How did she die, you ask?

This Is a Love Story

A man and his dog. In the wag of a tail he found the missing piece of an equation, the answer to the Sunday crossword. After obedience school, they were perfect for each other. He could have checked into the bridal suite at the ski lodge up the road. He kept the dog in the car though, and ordered two dinners, one to go. You know where it went.

When the morning failed to burn the mist off the hillside soon enough, the dog would go barking up the pasture, tearing it away with its body and voice, a hole in the white the man could walk through on his way into morning. At night he dreamed of the pressing hotness of dog fur and wrapped his arms around his wife's cool, hairless skin.

At the diner he told his friends he'd give his bed to his dog. This embarrassed them, but he was sincere and stared them down. A meal without the warm nudge of its body against his knee made the man nervous. He expected the failing blue of sunset to fall through the roof of the café, splintering like glass as it arrived. When he looked out the diner window, he could watch it watching him from the car. Balanced perfectly on haunches and front legs, it could have been his wife in the front seat.

He forgot where he'd left her. The perfect, moist circle of its breath on the windshield, the hieroglyph of pad and toes on the glass was something he had to stare through to drive. He saw the last red sun rays come at him like a fist his dog was riding on top of—in command—the tongue a spray of gladiola pink.

Was this unusual to find love at his age? To admit the strangeness of his wife? To find himself repeating the gestures he'd recently learned: throwing his head back and smelling the air as it came alive miles around him, noisy with scent, closing his eyes in the rainbow of smell that crowded him out of his skin? When they traveled, they always left the tent of human enterprise so far behind them. A man and his dog, on an invisible track that moved the dirt aside, pulled the birds down, swam them into the water and out again.

As the man smoked in the living room late at night, he watched the dark turn gray through the swirls, turn shapes, turn dog and lie down at his feet.

Historical Accuracy

He clipped the first one the weekend their parents caught up with them in Chicago and wouldn't let him admit her to The Home. It was theirs, too, and they would see to its care. Though he knew it was probably a lie, he was willing to go along with it. The idea of The Home had always bothered him. She had been certain it was the only thing to do. When she tried to kill herself in the motel room, he had gotten scared and called the adults in. Later, while she was recovering and he had nothing to do but wait for the flights to come in, he'd gone into the men's bathroom at the airport and taken off his tennis shoe, his wool sweat sock, and cut the big toenail he'd forgotten about until it had begun to nag at his shoe. It was at least an inch overgrown. None of the others seemed able to catch up with it. He hadn't even thought about throwing it away, but had placed it carefully in a piece of toilet paper he pulled from the roll in the stall he'd locked himself in, wrapped it up and put it in the very bottom of his chinos pocket. All day, through the negotiations with parents and, finally, the girl herself, whose belly had only begun to swell with their child, he'd fingered the sharp edge of nail.

Since he'd never lived so closely with another person, having to share the same bed (though she'd insisted on twin beds so she could push his away, they'd ended up tying the legs together) and having to share the same dresser, even (though she'd told him he'd only have two of the drawers for his very own), since all of this seemed to narrow things for him, it seemed natural that a month into their new marriage he would go out and buy himself a small metal box with a lock and key. He'd seen the box advertised in the Sunday paper as a good way to store valuables in the home. It seemed wise. She went along with it when he told her it was fireproof and placed in it the handwritten will they had each signed on notebook paper. They had given the child to someone else if they died. He was pretty sure she'd go before he did. After all, she'd already tried before. Other than that, she never tried to put anything in the strongbox. It seemed natural for him to begin to think of it as his own, for him to think of other things to store in there. But it seemed that the toenail might get lost just dropped in to rattle around with the paper of the will, so he purchased another box. This one was only an inch by an inch and plastic, black plastic. He liked the way the black set off the half-moon of toenail. It was impulse that made him take out his ballpoint pen and scratch a number *one* on the nail before he plinked it into the plastic box and put on the lid.

Five months later, the night his child was born, he again found himself, scissors in hand, sitting this time on the edge of the bed alone in their apartment, cutting the nail off the large toe of his right foot. The left seemed to stubble off or get clipped on a regular basis; it was only the right's stubborn growth that kept him fascinated. This one was a bit longer than number *one*, but also hornier, yellower. He took this as a sign and handled it with respect, carefully scratching number *two* across its ridges with his ballpoint pen's blue ink. Then he placed it under number *one* in the tiny black box, closed the lid, and placed the box back in its position under the notebook paper will, and now the black nylon underpants he had added to his collection of valuables. He had taken those home with him the first night they had made love that summer before she got pregnant, before they got married. She'd been scared and flattered by his gesture. What if her mother caught her without any underwear? Would he tell anyone else? They both knew he wouldn't. He picked up the panties, now wadded in a ball, and let them fall open, then raised them gently like a rose to his face and sniffed. Though the odor of their sweat had long ago disappeared, the feel of the material seemed to bring back the whole mystery of that night. If he closed his eyes, he could see her tan arms waving overhead like underwater plants, and hear the nothing that had roared in his head as he'd thrust and thrust inside of her. He was the largest she'd ever seen, she told him later; it hurt sometimes. He remembered the wild green smell of late August corn and alfalfa fields before the final cut; the creek that gurgled like syrup over the rocks as it dried in the heat, and the laziness of mosquitoes which hummed in their ears but for some reason didn't bite their sex-sweated bodies that hung halfway out the back seat of his mother's car. His father had been dead a month. He was not going back to school. He would stay and help his mother that fall with the business and his little sister. He was the only son. It was right.

Number *three* was the first time he let her know about the nails. And that was an accident really, though he hadn't tried to hide what he was doing. She was in the other room of the three-room apartment watching TV, the baby asleep, and he'd simply gotten out the scissors and the strongbox and sat down on the bed to perform the little ritual. They'd both been accepted to the University of Iowa to finish their college work and would be leaving their life there in Omaha, bounded by his mother on one side and her parents on the other. They seemed to have grown into a normal young couple with such watchfulness, and their baby was a normal young baby. Though it seemed to cry a lot, Dr. Spock assured them that was normal, too. Really, things couldn't be better, the adults told each other, and agreed to pay for the schooling that was near completion anyway.

At first he wasn't aware of her standing there in the doorway, watching him as he spread the box and its contents open on the edge of the bed. With all the precision of a jeweler, he removed the sock on his right foot, made sure the scissors were in working order, laid the ballpoint pen next to the little black plastic box that would hold number *three*. Her voice jarred him.

Later he forgave her for the laughter that had sent her rolling on the bed, messing things up, almost losing number *two* in the antics. Later still, he added the red underpants she had been wearing to the box, where, folded together with the black, they looked like a flag at rest. And again, later, he would remember number *three* as the night they had agreed to meet other people, to continue what had been interrupted by their untimely marriage and baby. It was all necessary to do, he'd explained to her, they wouldn't survive at their age without it. That was the third.

Sometime in the next year, he cut number *four,* but even he couldn't remember anything more about it. They were both so busy, seeing other people, keeping secrets, going to school. As it turned out, she was more popular than he was. Men gathered around her in the bars wherever she went. She had her heart broken and came home to tell him about it, both of them lying on the bed, like roommates. He told her about a girlfriend who had moved away, to make it even.

And again, six months later, he was on the bed in a different apartment, getting ready to cut the fifth, but she was in the kitchen taunting him, threatening to throw away the whole box because of what he'd done. Getting that poor, crazy girl pregnant, so her brother had to call and beg for money, and the girl was off wandering by the river threatening to jump in again. Two months later his wife asked him to leave so she could think. He didn't have a nail long enough to cut, so he took another pair of her underpants instead. These, he would smell over the long nights in the cement block cubicle he rented, not for the sexy odor, but for the clean laundry detergent scent from the weekly laundromat trip. His baby smelled the same way, and whenever he thought of this he started to cry.

It was almost a year before another nail grew long enough to trim. Something about the stress of his life then, he assumed later, but it scared him. He tried to write things down, but that was too complicated, too much had to be said. She had let him move back into the place with her after he'd started sleeping in the closet anyway. But it hadn't lasted. He tried taking pictures of her while she slept, or jumping out of doorways when she first woke up. He wanted to show her how he felt—how he was tired of other people. It hadn't worked. She wasn't tired of them, she told him. One day she rented another apartment and moved. She even left the baby with him. That was OK, it gave him something to do. That was number *six*.

For the next year he was too busy and too crazy to do anything but clip the toenail along with the rest every other week. With a baby and then a job and moving again, he had no time at all to think. He did manage to capture yet another pair of panties, this time from a girl he would later realize he should have married, but at the time, he wanted only her panties and her occasional presence in bed. When his wife tried to break it up, he took that as a sign and kept the girl around even more. His wife lost interest and filed for divorce. He filed, too. Things were still even that way.

In fact, it wasn't until another year later, when he delivered the child to his ex-wife, who had moved across the country to attend graduate school and get away from him, that he decided on number *seven*. He was seated in her fourth-floor apartment, big rooms in bad condition across from a factory, listening to the sounds of the woman giving their child a bath, getting to know the baby again after all that time. It was September and very hot at the top of the huge building clothed in metal stamped like gray stone. He had taken off his shoes and socks and was on the couch watching the sun go down across the tops of factories whose nineteenth-century New England roofs rose and fell like knuckles of a brown hand resting on the horizon. Something bit him on the leg, and it was the sharp sting of the nail itching the place that reminded him. Looking down at his foot, he saw that the nail, longer than ever before, almost glowed in the cooling light of dusk. He didn't have his scissors this time. Nor did he have the metal box which was tucked safely in the trunk of the car on the street below. But it was so long he figured ripping wouldn't damage it. He sat there a long time after that, holding number *seven* safely in his fist, watching the night gradually erase the world, and listening to the little songs his wife was singing in her flat little voice to their child's sleep. He hadn't planned it, but when he heard her footsteps finally in the kitchen, and the sound of her getting a beer from the fridge, he let his hand slide between the cushions and the back of the sofa, then pushed harder until he could feel the springs deep below, at the very spine of the chair, then he opened his hand and jiggled until he felt the sharp edge of number *seven* release his palm.

A Pleasant Story

It had happened quite by accident the Saturday Lucille was planting the geraniums. And she hadn't really missed it until a few days later, when it was too late to retrace her steps. Well, she thought to herself, there I go again, losing another one. No telling where this one might turn up, like the last time, in the washing machine, bedded like a lover with one of Arnold's socks. She had just sighed though, and reached into the drawer for another larger, less suitable one. Why was it always the smaller, handier ones that got lost first? You'd think I was tossing them out the windows here or something.

But she had continued fixing dinner that day, letting her mind turn to other things, planning the garden in back of the house, almost tasting the hot, salty tomatoes in her mouth come August. Sometimes she felt like her whole body would like nothing better than to stretch out there in the back like a vine and grow tomato red, little beads of dew glistening on her every morning.

Wouldn't Arnold be surprised at his tomato wife the first time he came to bed and she wasn't there? Then he'd call all over the house, even down to the laundry room to see if she wasn't catching up on some washing or ironing, but not a sight of her. (She chuckled to herself as she sliced some cucumber for the salad.) And then he'd probably wander out back, stumbling a little in his bare feet and pajamas. Why, he'd look like a drunk, she thought, chuckling again, with his head thrust forward like a parrot, a nearsighted parrot, peering into the dark with his eyes all squinty. He wouldn't want the neighbors to hear, so he'd be half whispering, half calling, and his voice would go hoarse with the effort. "Lucille," he'd call, "Lucille are you out here?"

She'd catch a little twinge of anger in his voice because he wouldn't be able to find her, and then she'd have to roll around a little, make a rustling noise in her vine shape so he could. Pretty soon he'd be standing right over her, seeing her for the first time, demanding that she get right out of that garden and come inside before the neighbors saw her and called the police. Maybe she'd pop a hard green tomato at him then, just a joke, pop it like a button into his face, then laugh at his surprise as he rubbed the spot on his cheek.

"Now that's enough, Lucille. You come in here right now, get out of those tomatoes. I've had enough of this . . ."

But she'd roll around a bit more and he'd realize that she wasn't coming in to bed that night, and go off, panting to himself, walking gingerly, not wanting to hurt his bare feet.

"Lucille, is dinner ready?" She could hear Arnold's voice from the other room, where he was reading the paper.

"Yes, dear, in a few minutes." That sure would be a joke on him—make him sit up and think, to have her become a tomato vine.

A few days later she noticed a new plant among the geraniums and nettles in the garden. It didn't look familiar, and at first she was inclined to weed it out, but then she thought to herself, why not give it a week or so longer, it wasn't hurting anything and it might turn out nice. She was always taking chances with the garden. She lacked the organization of her neighbor, who knew what everything looked like, knew exactly where weeds and flowers grew. In fact, her neighbor always leaned over the redwood fence that separated their yards and gave her advice until Lucille wished that fence would suddenly give way and her neighbor would land like a fat squirrel in the wild mustard she was letting dominate the garden. (Then Lucille could chase it around with her rake, give it a good scare.) "The wild mustard has nice yellow flowers," she told her neighbor's humpf. Lucille was a gambler in the garden. She bet on every hand, every weed. It was roulette and there was always a chance—the slightest one at that—that the plant would unfold itself into something wonderful, beautiful, mutated even with the others, an emissary between flower, vegetable and weed worlds.

Arnold just shook his head when she pointed out the strange plant among the geraniums, "You know I don't know anything about this stuff. Grow vegetables, I told you before, something practical."

When Lucille finally pointed it out to her neighbor, the woman's high, cracked laugh let her know immediately that it was another failure. She looked with disgust and longing at the neatly ordered dahlias, iris, gloxinias across the fence, then to the patchy scene in front of her— bits of weeds and a couple of elm seedlings struggling up the middle of daisies, columbine, geraniums, all too close together, underwatered, underfed. She was of a mind to let everything go to seed this year, blow across the fence and teach her neighbor a lesson.

"I don't care. I think I'll see what it turns out to be. No harm in that—I like surprises." Lucille had answered the laugh with a resolute stab of her hand spade into the dirt. When it struck something, she kept digging, then pulled out a bit of metal—something broken off of a machine, a cog or wheel, thick with rust. "What's this doing here?"

"Oh, people used to plant those in the garden, anything metal, to provide minerals for the soil. I find things like that all the time . . . when I'm cultivating." She said this last with a particular tone that implied something more like "when you're not cultivating," but Lucille let it go. She had something in store for the neighbor later that day. A friend of hers from the country was bringing in a truckload of horse manure for her gardens. It would smell to high heaven, and her neighbor would have to wear a scarf over her nose to do any gardening for the next two weeks. It delighted Lucille.

A month later the plant had assumed the straight, hard stalk of a tree and begun to leaf out. Lucille was content to let it be. It didn't hurt anything except her neighbor, who glanced at it maliciously each time she tended the garden on her side of the fence. And when Lucille was outside, the neighbor would usually hustle out the back door, wiping her hands on the apron she always wore as she came to the fence, almost breathless with advice. "That's a tree you know, a tree!"

"What kind do you think it is?" Lucille knew this would stump her. She had been through all her books on trees and gardening for the Western United States, and she couldn't find it. Maybe a tree seed from the Eastern United States had accidentally blown over the Mississippi and landed here. It was hard to know what to do about those books when you lived on the dividing line the way she did. You couldn't buy both sections, it was too expensive, yet it did make sense that some seeds could migrate or that birds could drop them off. She had heard of that. Birds as seeders—it was a nice idea and she quit disliking the bird droppings on the garage roof after she had thought about it.

The neighbor put her finger to her cheek, cradled her elbow with her other hand and took a long, withering look at the plant. It almost rustled under her hard gaze. "A Japanese mock orange . . . no, a false widow's willow . . . or a prickly striped basswood." She paused, then nodded her head wisely, "Take my word, it's one of those and it will make a mess out of this . . . this garden if you leave it here. Trees are a nuisance. We took the birch out because it was only supposed to grow to five feet, a miniature they told us, then it shot right up to eight feet and started shading everything in sight. So I had my husband take it right out of there. "No more trees," I told him, "enough is enough." You'd better have Arnold dig that out right away or it will take over everything."

Lucille remembered the birch. First they had tried topping it off so that it stood like a decapitated body for a few months, thick and oozing life out the stumps, until, finally, its ugliness brought it to the end and she had awoken at eight o'clock one Saturday morning to the buzz of the saw. The neighbors always did major work as early as possible.

Lucille tossed some more horse manure on the tree; it seemed to like the care it was getting because it was growing faster than anything else in the garden. She had even replanted the rusted cog beside the tree and, since, had added other bits of broken metal.

When it reached four feet in August, it began to bud out, like a fruit tree in April. Again the growth seemed remarkable, but Lucille put it down to the extra care, the horse manure and the metal pieces. It was comforting to see it rising above the fence line, waving gently in the summer breezes, and once in a while she caught a glint of something silvery in its leaves, which were long and dagger-shaped. The tree pleased her. Arnold, of course, had taken the neighbor's side of it. "Cut it down," he ordered.

"I don't think so," she replied, tossing an extra dash of pepper into the mashed potatoes.

"Watch what you're doing there."

"Then don't distract me while I'm cooking—go read the paper, or take a walk. The tree stays." Arnold was surprised by Lucille's tone, but obeyed her. Sometimes Lucille was very surprising.

One morning Lucille was startled out of bed by the phone. She had gone back to sleep after Arnold left and now felt clumsy with tiredness as she fumbled for the receiver.

"I tried to trim that part that's reaching over the fence to my side, but I can't. What is that thing?" It was her neighbor's indignant voice.

"What?"

"What is that tree? It broke the shears and cut my fingers trying to pull off the leaves. I told you so—it's starting to shade my garden and I can't get it to stop!" The neighbor's voice was rising hysterically, like a mother pig's squeal, Lucille thought, running in circles that voice.

She yawned and answered, "I'll be out in a few minutes to see what I can do." Honestly, that woman needed to get a job, a hobby, children.

Looking out the window as she dressed, Lucille could see the friendly wave of the tree as it dipped across the fence, its fruit now long green stems about as thick as her fingers. They looked like tadpoles, taking on more and more definition as they ripened. It looked so restful down there among the squash in her garden this time of year. She often wanted to curl up under the broad leaves, snuggle into the warm, moist shade beside the zucchinis and crooknecks and take a nap. Imagine Arnold finding her there, head resting comfortably in the curved cushion of the squash, a yellow blossom at her throat, dinner forgotten. He'd know she was there by her feet sticking out from the patch, the shoes resting at the edge of the garden. Now that would be fun, she giggled—Arnold demanding that she get out of the squash immediately. The neighbor lady looking arch and knowing from her kitchen window. When she woke up, she knew she'd start laughing at the sight of Arnold, the leaves over her face would bounce up and down with the gasping. Lucille almost laughed out loud as she pulled on her shoes.

Outside, her neighbor waited, angrily tapping her foot, arms on her hips. This is serious, Lucille thought. When the woman saw Lucille, she started waving a bandaged hand at her. "See, see what that tree did to me? Worse than barberry—worse than anything. Cut right into my fingers, sliced them neat as you please."

Lucille apologized for the tree and looked at the cuts when the neighbor exposed them. Really, it was a bit much for first thing in the morning. They reminded her of the sort she got fixing dinner. Walking around the tree for a few minutes, she thought how nicely it was coming along. And it only reached across the fence a little bit. She didn't want to spoil its shape by lopping off one side. She'd have to placate the neighbor. "It's not really shading your side yet. Let it go until fall and I'll have Arnold get to it then. You can have a cutting off my President Lincoln lilac if you want." The neighbor and the tree nodded simultaneously.

A week later she discovered the first one. It was a bright morning in late August. The neighbor must have been gone, because she didn't come out of the house to bother Lucille as she worked in the garden. Arnold was at work. The tree's fruit was clearly beginning to mature, and when she had examined the tree that day, she had found it on the ground at its base. A paring knife. Just like the one she had left in the ground when she had planted geraniums way back in May. She remembered it then. Of course, that was where the knife had gone to; she had used it to cut back the long stems as she transplanted. Although she knew she should use her pruning shears, she always just picked up a paring knife from the kitchen to work with the plants. Now wasn't that something! She had turned it over in her palm and noted how nicely the metal glinted in the light and how fresh the wood handle looked. You'd never know it had spent all those months underground. She ran right into the house then and tried it out. It worked beautifully, just like its old self.

A few mornings later, when Lucille was weeding the begonias, her neighbor stepped around to the fence with an object clutched in her extended hand. "Here, you must have left this on the post there, where the wind could blow it over. It was in my garden by the coralbells this morning." It looked like the knife Lucille had lost and found earlier, only she didn't remember using it the day before.

Startled, she took the knife without protest. "Yes, uh, thanks. I've been missing that," she lied. Lucille was pretty sure she knew where it had come from. Later that same day, she spotted another with its tip neatly buried like an ostrich head in the iris, only the brown wooden handle gave it away. It was handy finding them this way, she reflected; summers were usually her worst season for losing knives.

On the following day she woke up early and went out to inspect the yard carefully. Sure enough. There were paring knives in other places, lying carelessly in shrubs or sticking out of deep grasses in shady corners, as if all the knives she had ever lost were now turning up at once. All day she thought about it, the surprise of it. When Arnold came home she would pull him, eyes closed, to the back yard. Once in front of the tree, she would command him to open his eyes. "What do you see?" she'd ask him.

"The same tree that has been driving us all nuts this summer."

"Look closer," she'd urge him, "what do you see?"

With this, he would lean closer and examine the fruit; some others were beginning to ripen. "No, no, this is one of your games, isn't it, this couldn't be . . ." He would protest, but she would insist.

"Yes, it is. It's a knife tree! I accidentally buried the paring knife here last spring and it sprouted. Isn't that great?" In her fantasy, Lucille could see that it wasn't great to Arnold; he just shook his head. She'd never be able to convince him.

Lucille's knife tree grew with phenomenal speed, and by the next year its branches were tapping metallically against the dining-room windows. Lucille didn't mind though, because although it was spreading out to cover the whole yard and garden, its silvery thin leaves didn't really shade anything. Even the neighbor couldn't complain, except when the fruit ripened and the clatter on her sidewalk kept her awake at night and made her afraid to walk outside during the day. But Lucille took the initiative and went around with bushel baskets and gloves and picked them all up so that no one would get hurt. The neighbor's husband would get up each morning to inspect the backyard for the alleged attack of noise the night before and find nothing. He began to worry about his wife's sleeplessness.

Arnold, on the other hand, was pleased that Lucille was finally showing some energy by getting up early each day to work in the garden. The only thing that bothered him was that by the third year, the tree was peeking in the upstairs bedroom window and he was worried that one of the sharp limbs would poke through the screens. There was this other problem, too, but he had decided not to speak to Lucille just yet. It seemed that over the past few years she had started collecting paring knives, and now they filled all the drawers in the kitchen, and boxes of them had started appearing in the hall closet, the attic and the basement. He was afraid to look under the bed, because he thought he had seen the metallic wink of a blade the other day when he had been looking for a lost shoe there. A few months ago when he had casually mentioned the fact that instead of losing them now, she seemed to be finding them—more than her share to be sure—Lucille had just laughed and tossed her head. "It's the knife tree out back," she had smiled mysteriously as she peeled a radish into a perfect little rose. Well, it was just another surprise in Lucille, Arnold thought. It seemed harmless enough. A knife tree indeed.

On the other hand, he probably would have to chop it down one of these days. A few weeks ago he had noticed that there were holes in the roof caused by limbs dragging across it during storms. And lately he had noticed some seedlings starting up around the yard from fruit she had missed; at least she claimed she had missed them, but you couldn't tell about Lucille all the time—after all, she had said that she was growing a knife tree. But he would explain it all to her, and she'd be reasonable. The lawnmower couldn't cut through those seedlings, and the roof—well, they just couldn't afford to get a whole new roof for the sake of one tree. She'd understand.

During the winter everything went along fine because the knife tree was dormant. Oh, once in a while Lucille would pick out the silvery glint of a residual fruit in the thin wintry light, but generally things were pretty calm. The backyard looked like anyone else's on their street. Even the neighbor's.

Then the next summer, the fourth year, things started to take off in a little different direction. Lucille, for her part, was as happy as ever, gardening, putting out little pieces of metal to fertilize the tree and little bits of seed for the birds that hopped around the yard. She was aware, though, that her neighbor eyed her angrily from her kitchen window, afraid of her own backyard these days, what with the tree and all. Her garden was a mess, too. She just couldn't work up enough courage to get out there and go at it with all that commotion overhead. Who could blame her, she muttered to herself. At night when her husband came home, tired and worried from work, she threatened him with lawsuits and divorce unless he did something about that tree next door. It was a public menace—who knew where it would end? And now they couldn't even have people over because their yard was such a wreck, the perennial beds a mass of waving grasses, nightshade twining around peonies, roping them to the ground almost, and she wasn't going to take her life in her hands and go out there. No sir, she still had a scar on her palm from the last time. Her husband just eyed her with quiet resignation and wondered if it would be worth it to sneak across the fence some night, chop down the tree, and get some peace and quiet for a change.

But nothing really happened until August, when the neighbor finally found a course of action. Lucille had spent the morning in the garden, enjoying the solitude without her neighbor's advice, digging and fertilizing before it got too hot. She liked the way she had to dress now that harvest time was here again—a pith helmet she had gotten at a yard sale protecting her head, a short fur coat (figuring that the animal hide would resist better than cloth), and a flak jacket she had saved up to buy out of the grocery money last year (wouldn't Arnold be surprised!). On her legs she wore goalie pads she had picked up secondhand from an ex-hockey star turned advertising executive. Whenever Lucille gardened in this outfit, she imagined her neighbors warning their children to stay away from her—she *was* an odd one.

She'd like to keep bees in this outfit, she thought—drop a piece of netting over her head, pull on the goalie mitts she'd gotten with the leg protectors, and lift the cores of the hives out. Soaking with honey, they would glisten and tumble over her hands clumsy in the gloves studded on the back with sharp metal stars. The bees, furry with sleep and work, would crawl up her arms, and she'd get right into the hive with them, bury herself in the sweet thickness of their hum. And Arnold would come home that night, tired from work, impatient for dinner, and unable to find her anywhere in the house amidst the still-growing collection of knives, he would come stumbling out into the dazzling late sun in the backyard. "Lucille, Lucille, you come out of there now—I'm afraid of the bees," he'd call to her from the safety of several yards away. Her laughing would erupt as an angry buzz of startled bees. "Oh, Arnold, you should try this once," she'd want to call to him, but her throat so thick with honey . . .

In the afternoon, when Lucille was taking her nap, a big storm started building, the way they do in that part of the country, the air swirling with dust and leaves tearing from trees. What awakened her, though, wasn't the sound of the wind or the tree limbs that had begun digging into the roof. It was the grinding buzz of an electric drill or saw, something that was coming from somewhere behind her house. She paused in her drowsiness for a few minutes, the way she always did, to locate the noise, to reassure herself that it was in the outside world and not coming from some dream. Then suddenly she knew. Leaping out of bed with nothing but the sheet clutched around her bare body, she ran to the window looking out over the backyard. Yes, there it was—a truck whose motor ran roughly under the whine and grind of the saw that the man was pressing directly against a larger limb of her knife tree that stretched out to her neighbor's lawn through the overhead wires. She gasped as the watched the saw sink dramatically all at once up to its edge, the limb giving way suddenly to its bite. Then the man, middle aged, balding, dressed in some sort of tan uniform or utility clothes, pulled the saw away. Next he attacked a small limb hanging out over the alley where his truck was parked. That limb, too, gave way easily. When he noticed Lucille watching him, he waved, pointed to the sign on the side of his truck, turned and got in behind the wheel and drove away. The sign had said Northern States Power Company.

Despite the thunder and lightning that now started booming across the neighborhood, Lucille quickly dressed and ran downstairs and outdoors to check on the tree. It creaked and groaned overhead, as she inspected the wound on the trunk, the gap in the branches; and when she turned to look at her neighbor's house for a moment, she thought she heard a crack of wood giving way, just as she caught a glimpse of her neighbor's figure moving away from the window.

It was awfully upsetting for Lucille. The doctor had to be called, and Arnold couldn't do much but sit around holding her limp hand, his face all white and soggy with worry. It was only a mild concussion and she'd have to take it easy for a few weeks; she'd be OK, he reassured Arnold. The next morning when Arnold called Northern States Power, they told him there had been a report that the tree was rubbing power lines and that the inspector had just been checking to see if there was a danger of it taking down any wires. In fact, it turned out that the tree was rotting from the inside out. Unusual, yes, but not unheard of in trees that reached maturity rapidly. By the way, the person had asked Arnold, what kind of tree was it, just for the record. Arnold thought for a minute, then answered, "A Knife Tree."

The Man of Sorrows

It wasn't that he was afraid of using the telephone; he'd done that most of his life. It only happened occasionally. He never knew for sure, as he picked up the receiver, whether his index finger would remain frozen in the hole of the first digit. He usually preferred the old-style phone with holes, saddles for his fingers to ride through the sometimes ordeal of dialing. With those newer phones—the push buttons, for instance—there was nothing to *hold* the finger onto the phone—no real connection made there. A man could slip off one of those little squares marked G4HI onto T8UV or # or into space itself. Forever. No contact. Just as fearful, of course, but in a different way, was chance—and chance here was not to be discounted, confused with coincidence, accident, grand design or a cosmos of random factors. No. It was the chance, the possibility of reaching the inevitable "wrong number." He had entire books on the subject in his mind. Lengthy discourses argued in the leisure of an hour's bath or the preparation of a breakfast in his tiny Pullman-style kitchen. The stove, too ancient to be efficient but built into its niche permanently by the younger-day enthusiasm of the landlord, required time as its payment. Then, too, he would argue between bites of his morning toast and egg—a man who ate a traditional breakfast at 7 A.M. each day.

The wrong number, first of all, would mean that one of several possibilities had occurred, willy-nilly. No amount of bathing or breakfasting had resolved the exact cause-effect for him, so he had, over the years, progressed to the next aspect of the problem: how. First, the pure leap of faith performed by his own finger, which unwatched could be counted on to stumble en route from one hole to another. He had never been able to dial the phone in the dark, for instance, as he'd seen people do in movies or watched his infrequent lovers do after lovemaking, ignoring the length of his body, his legs particularly something he was proud of. They wouldn't see them in the dark, webbed with muscle and bone. No, they simply reached for the phone, knowing it to be right where it should, and dialed in the dark, the finger hitting each hole correctly, sensing the numbers distributed appropriately along the circle. Or even more startling to him, they would punch out the number on the push buttons, the little melody of response an assurance of their own rightness in this world. No, he felt far away from that. His fingers lacked that assurance, that absolute reliability. And he could even touch type. No, he had never penetrated the mystery of dialing.

Even when he performed his end of things perfectly— dialing slowly, as advised in the phone use pages in the front of the book. (What idiot did not know how to dial a phone in this society? Children—mere infants—seemed born with an innate ability, their cultural inheritance, to dial the telephone.) He had carefully read the simple instructions. At one time, he had gone to the telephone company and presenting a story about research into early telephone history, had gained entrance into their private library which contained, as he knew it would, telephone books and instruction manuals from all time. These he spent days pouring over, returning each morning during his vacation, practicing at night the techniques described in the books, placing his index finger just so. Now he was careful never to attempt dialing with any other finger. Only the index would do—had the proper strength and angle. Any other finger could result in a misdial. Perhaps that accounted also for his stubborn reliance on the old-style phone—he was traditionalist in company parlance.

At the end of his study he knew he had mastered the phone-dialing technique, but like learning to play tennis by correspondence, there existed a gap between scientific knowledge and performance. Style remained another question.

But it remained mysterious, also, that should he complete his performance precisely, if a bit clumsily, there existed that chance of mistake—that horrible moment of hearing the Whitby Elevator Company's receptionist in nasal tones. Or worse yet, that prolonged embarrassment, the wrong number haggle: "Who's this?" "No who's this?"—compounded at times by reaching someone with exactly the first name of the person he was trying to call. Or a child—that was awful—appearing on the other end of the line, leaving him in helplessness and despair as he repeated over and over his simple request: "get mom-my, me hold, don't, don't hang up . . ."

At times he discovered that the phone company inadvertently crossed its wires, so that no matter how many times he dialed Julie, he got Mort Smith, who, growing angrier with every assault, left him feeling a bit triumphant. For once he was in the right, he would pursue Mort across time and space—through the black rubber-coated lines stringing their houses together. He would not let old Mort off the hook. He would insist in his most aggressive manner that Mort talk to him, repeat his denial over and over, "No, this is the wrong number," so that *he* could reply, "I am certain that I dialed correctly; yes, I know, but is

Julie there?'' This usually sent his newfound connection into a frenzy of curses, which delighted him. Finally, when Mort refused to answer the phone anymore, he would report the mix-up to the company. This usually left him feeling a little empty; somehow that power to change the lines back to their correct latitude and longitude depressed him more than anything. A mere click of a switch, a slight one-eighth turn of a screw, and Mort Smith was back in his own life. And he in his. When he dialed the next time, barring all other chance factors, Julie would indeed be on the other end, and he would feel a little sad.

On the other hand, there also existed the possibility with each completed dial of reaching the phone company itself—via its vast repertoire of taped messages. He actually felt ambivalent about this occurrence. At times it amused him to hear that voice admonishing him, mildly enough, to dial again, to check with his operator, to use a long distance code, or informing him that his friends had disappeared into thin air—the out-of-order/disconnected message. He could see their figures receding into the distance, finally evaporating into the vapor beyond—a modern miracle he rather enjoyed. Usually he responded with a smile, a wave, and a long, respectful apostrophe in the relationship—waiting appropriately until their return to the world. But on other occasions he became enraged or, worst of all, cowed by the voice—not the one he wanted at all. He could, at such moments, be driven to yell at the recorded voice, summoning all his rancor in extended curses, using all his phone lore to cut through the mechanical voice, to burn his anger into the very cells of the wires, to activate their molecular structure with his acid tongue. He was certain that someday he would break it all down, that he would bring that voice to life, give it the violent birth of his anger.

But in moments of humility, chastened by the condescension of the tape reminding him of his own fault, however karmic it was, he knew that he was responsible. Correct dial or not. Had his friends moved away? Relocated? Dislocated? Disjunctured? GONE OUT OF ORDER—GONE OUT OF TOWN? It was his fault—christ, he was sorry. His voice stumbled apologies across the wires, a Morse code of old. The fluid communication gone, he would break the wires into thousands, millions of pieces with the staccato of his embarrassed replies. Then he would hang up the phone in great sorrow—too agonized, too responsible to check with his operator, to call information.

He would do penance for his misdeeds, waiting for days until he returned to the phone, until he had cleansed himself thoroughly of his evil. He would stare longingly at the phone book, placed knowingly on its little wooden telephone stand, but be unable to touch it until he had purified himself, admitted his stupidity, his ultimate culpability in the universe, his striving for telephone perfection broken at the roots, like a young tree stubbed off near the ground. How could he begin again? After a few days (the most he'd gone without dialing had been twelve days—he considered that a perfect number, though it did not exist on the face of the telephone), he would again return to the phone, dial, and with great joy and relief, usually get his number. Then he was flooded with gratitude and release. He had been redeemed.

It happened that this morning he had to make a phone call. Moreover, it happened that this was complicated by the fact that he was indeed at the end of one of his periods of abstinence. Like St. John, crawling out of the desert after weeks without food and water, but in the clutches of a great vision and a great cleansing of the spirit, he was weak in the face of this impending renewal of dealings with the outside world. What if . . . but no, he wouldn't let himself go through that again. Instead he would think positively, as they advised in magazine articles these days.

He recalled that ten years ago, of course, all the articles said to give up the self, let go of the ego, give give give and ye shall receive. Now as he read the signs of the times in drugstores or supermarket checkout lines (he had developed the art of the quick scan), he was supposed to repossess his dispossessed self: that evil-ridden ego could be housed once more in his own body. No more denial and selfless love. Now he was to be the man with the clenched fist, the man with a glint in his eye and a tough smile on his lips—not that ironic, self-indulgent smile of old, the man too good or too tired to dirty his hands with the world, but that man who could carry a briefcase and make it look like a club. The man in the well-tailored suit; the man with a clean, styled haircut. One who closed deals, barked orders, and knew HIMSELF and GOT WHAT HE WANTED—the man who *thought* positively. That was who he must try to be today. He would practice.

As he breakfasted at his small oak table, pushed, as it had to be, against the wall and framing the tiny kitchen, he felt the weight of the phone. It sat sternly on its table now. It, too, had its power this morning. The telephone seemed to glow with all the power of positive thinking in the world. It was the purity of form itself—no extras, no nonsense—yet not afraid to have a good time. No, he would not think of that, he hadn't done that in a long time—after all, what was to be gained? The telephone was, the company book reassured him, an instrument of supreme convenience—a tool to insure the successful completion of his business, his leisure, his social life. It was one of his modern servants. He didn't have to know how to write anymore. He could even ship via his telephone, never leaving his apartment. Everything could be brought to his door. Let your fingers do the walking, they advised. Yes, that was it: the telephone as servant—just the right note. That put HIM in control. Now he could wait, make the call at his leisure. Hell, he could take a bath,

read a book, anything—and suddenly, when he felt like
it, in the very midst of lovemaking even, reach over, pick
up that squat black body and make the call. Nothing to it.
When he realized that he was pacing the four feet of
his living room, coffee cup cooling between his hands,
he walked to the windows siding one end of the apartment, opposite the kitchen. Fine. The sun was out. It
would probably reach 65 degrees today. After his phone
call he could go out bicycling. The elms lining the alleys
and streets in his neighborhood were beginning to leaf
out at last. Outside his building the elms arched the
street—a special effect created through the careful pruning by men who arrived each spring and fall in orange
city trucks equipped with long basket cranes a man could
stand in, protected from disaster by a railing and wire mesh
to his waist. From his safe perch he could clip the year's
growth of new branches or the older dying ones which
drooped unsymmetrically. Only the Dutch elm disease had
thus far defeated the formality of this arrangement
between the city and nature. Even when it became appar-
ent that the elm limbs might snap the telephone wires
strung tentatively through their very tops, a compromise
was created to maintain the cathedral vaulting over the
local streets and to preserve the sanctity of communication. It seemed never to have occurred to any of the men
involved on either side that underground cables would
have served just as well. And so it was that the trees on
one side of some streets had achieved a peculiar shape
which seemed almost grotesque to him. The very heart,
the center of the canopy of huge old elms, had been
carved out—as if a wedge had been cleanly inserted and
withdrawn, the wound cauterized by the lines which now
dissected the middle of each tree. Thus the city had its
effect, since the trees on each side spreading luxuriously
over and into each other continued to shade the streets
in a monumental fashion. The telephone company

retained its autonomy, with the all-important lines moving straight along from one point to another without hindrance. Only the absurd appearance of the trees themselves remained as testimony. But he knew all this. He had watched them pruning the same trees for several seasons, in the same fashion, for the same reason. It had almost stopped troubling him. He was even beginning to feel philosophical about it now. He rather enjoyed the comfort of seeing those wires race through every obstacle, deterred by nothing, a sure and positive sign of the rightness of technology.

What did trouble him now was the dirt he saw on his windows, or rather through them. He would have to clean those windows before he did anything else, including the phone call, but then that could wait, he knew. Nine o'clock was probably too early to call. Ten always seemed like a more cordial time for phoning—less likely to get a yawning hello or an annoyed yes. No morning sex to interfere with—hell, if they were doing it at ten in the morning, what did they expect? But he would have to wash those windows, four of them, before anything else could happen that day. Maybe he had never washed them. He couldn't remember exactly, had he? Well, in that case, he'd have to do both inside and outside. OK. One last glance outside, sun shining, etc. Everything right. Wires all balanced and parallel. Trees waving rhythmically in the slight breeze. It was just fine for washing windows. Call later.

As he poured Spic and Span into his yellow plastic pail, followed by water as hot as he could stand, he thought again of the phone call. The problem, as he saw it, (and he always did see it, of course), lay partly in the type of phone call one made. Was it a chatty note to a friend? That, given all that could go wrong, was not too hard. Or a brief exchange of information, even, could be handled skillfully at times, with some suaveness. But today, today he had the most loathsome of telephone tasks. Yes, that was it. He turned off the water, noticing that the scalding sensation seemed both hot and cold on his skin as he plunged his hand in to search for the sponge. He always had that experience with water: either his senses were somewhat askew or, more probably, he figured, the linguistic description of hot and cold was too limited. Otherwise, how could an experience of either extreme create a physical reaction of its opposite?

Just as he set down the pail of burning water, the phone gave a slight burp, frightening him so that he almost stepped into the pail, the toe of his shoe at the point of entry as he jumped back. Goddamn it. Why did it always frighten him? And why did it do that? Not a real ring, which although admittedly startled him, he could deal with as if the prolonged sound stabilized his fear. The other, however, those small electronic urps, which came out of the black box infrequently, always threw him off balance. They seemed more an intrusion than the ringing. He knew from experience that no one was there. He had picked up the phone often enough, said hello to the voiceless buzz on the line, humiliated himself in a thousand ways to that belch of a phone—that tentative leap of connection, uncompleted. What was it, he demanded at times. A friend changing his mind? A million dollars almost won? A wrong number? A wrong life? What the hell was it?

There was no company information on this strange occurrence. No company personnel were willing to even discuss it. They passed it off or ignored it, claiming at different times that it didn't even happen, at others, readily admitting the occasional chance ring, a single relay of recognition from the world. No, he knew better than to fall into *that* trap. At any rate, he was never really prepared for that sound, but had disciplined himself to control the situation to some degree by refraining from picking up the phone. There would be no one there. Once or twice there had been someone there after a false ring, but that was only a chance factor, a come-on he wasn't falling for, no matter how his fingers tingled to grip the smooth plastic, his tongue articulating the sounds of hello. No. He had figured it out.

Over ninety-nine percent of those truncated signals were false alarms, mere testings of his reflexes, and for a while he had entertained the notion that, furthermore, the company sent them out periodically, at random, of course—he wasn't paranoid for chrissakes—to instill and to maintain a near Pavlovian response in the nervous systems of the telephone subscribers—to maintain high performance in the telephone user. In case a particular number was not called often or had alienated itself suffi- ciently to merit only rare calls, the burping noise would provide stimulus-response training, as well as a gentle reminder of companionship. However, its effect on him was usually more startling than companionable—in fact, he often felt an incalculable longing after such an erup- tion. It made him want to receive a call, or, more accurately, it made him want to make a call. Perhaps *that* was the company's notion after all, he couldn't be sure.

When he had regained his balance, wiped the tip of his shoe off (it was only a little soapy but he couldn't walk that stuff all over the floor), he stood for a minute staring at the phone. It was waiting patient enough, steady, like an animal tied to a post, its small body hunched down on the dark wooden stand. Its face, scored with numbers, wore that look, a mixture of ignorance and pride. A secret revealed or concealed: pick a number, any number. He knew that old game. He'd tried that, it was a sucker's game: Hello? Hello? The old allure though, that beckon- ing come-hither look: "Come on, big boy," it seemed to whisper, "just breathe into my ear . . ."

No, no. He wasn't going back into *that*—he could do something later, but not now, and not that. He felt the stirrings in his pants and gripped the sponge he had pulled out for the windows even tighter. Later, he insisted. No, now, it urged. No later, afterwards. The phone was for business now. No, pleasure. No chance meetings along its dark tunneling through the town. No dark ladies, no dark voices. No.

He looked away, back to the four windows. First he would wash them inside with the soapy mixture (that would feel good, his pants told him), then rinse, then dry with yesterday's paper. Finally, he would have to repeat the process on the outside of each window. Christ, he hoped the phone didn't ring while he was stuck on the ledge three stories up—he'd probably fall out the damn window. He could unplug the phone, or take it off the hook, but that seemed unfair, somehow like cheating. No, he'd have to play the game fairly. If he fell, well, that was that. But in all his dealings with the telephone, he had come to see it as a necessary, if chance, element in his universe. His resolve wilted the enthusiasm in his pants as he set to work on the windows.

It happened, in fact, that no one had called him in at least two weeks. It could even have been three, he wasn't positive, but he was certain that for at least ten to fourteen days, he had not heard the phone ring. He was not particularly anxious about this. He had himself refrained from using the phone. It was an agreement of sorts between himself and the world. He sat in his two rooms serving as four, and the world continued at an agreeable distance in its appropriate space. Now, however, he had to make a call. The thought nagged at him, as it had since waking. He had pondered the issue through breakfast, carefully chewing each bite to the rhythm of the key question, devouring the words, feeling them settle in his stomach, later to pump his blood back and forth through the morning. How to leap the hurdles of the moment of hello. Hello? This is? Say his name? Theirs?

He finished the inside windows in half an hour, even working as slowly as he could. Chasing each droplet of water off the sill, out of the corner. He had done it perfectly. Now he must open the window, hoist himself and the bucket out, then sit on the ledge, feet and legs dangling inside, back to the open space behind him, and wash the windows outside. This he did again in a slow, measured way, listening to the various sounds of the day outside his apartment—children, cars in the street, birds, and the wind occasionally tapping branches against the building. He did not glance down. That wouldn't do. He was, moreover, careful that his sleeve neither dipped into the water as he rinsed the sponge nor housed the dirty dribblings of water which ran down his arm once in a while. Always he thought of the call. He tried to imagine it. The voice a woman's, he hoped, asking a question, "Do you . . . ?"

By the time he had finished the windows, all four inside and out, it was ten-thirty. The outside had taken longer because it was done in a more awkward position. He had had to be relatively careful not to make any sudden jarring, unbalancing movements. He was glad that the phone had not rung or burped—he liked that word, which seemed to accurately describe the sense he got of the machine eating and digesting his words as fact, as novel information stored in fatty tissue or burned off immediately.

Finally he knew it was time to make the call. He had to do it before the other party left for an early luncheon or tennis or shopping or whatever other people did with the middle of their days. As he climbed back through the last window, he was careful not to kick over his single plant stationed on the floor. It was a large, two-armed affair with an infinite number of tiny spines that seemed to leap into his fingers or pant legs almost by suggestion. He swore that on several occasions he had not even touched the damn thing, but had found the minute slivers bristling painfully from his palm anyway. Now he harbored a growing dislike for the plant, but was unable, as yet, to imagine the mechanics of its destruction. After the safe negotiation back into his living room and the disposal of his cleaning implements—no reason a man living alone should not keep his place clean and neat. Men weren't all that bad, he reassured himself, awarding that special sense of virtue every time he managed to maintain his level of tidiness. He enjoyed being tidy. He liked that word, too, *tidy*—it fit nicely into a certain view he had.

After all of these maneuvers, he was finally ready to make the call. Yes, there was the telephone. Established. Its face blank and receptive. He stood now in the living room, hands deep in pockets, legs together, toes straight. This was his moment of truth, a trivial enough moment to some, he knew, but to him, the moment which ultimately controlled his destiny, his being (he liked to couch matters in such terms, perhaps his one concession to the spiritual life. He was careful not to mention these ideas to other people).

As he stood before the phone now, fingers tensing to grip the receiver, voice churning in his throat, stomach tossing slowly over the morning eggs and toast, he felt a movement from below his belt. His pants seemed to stretch tighter between his pocketed hands, and he became aware now of another feeling welling up from between his legs. First, the small pulsings pleasant enough, reminders of another world, which seemed to obliterate, to literally wipe out this one. Then he knew the slight ache from the pressure of his chino pants—signal for release. He touched himself gently with his left hand, pressing his fingers through the thin cotton dacron of the pocket. He loved the feel of it, flexing at each touch like the muscled arms of the athletes he watched on TV. The phone, meanwhile, seemed to recede a little from his vision. The tightness in his pants, he knew, would have to be resolved first. He would have to go into his small bedroom/office, the second of his two rooms, yes, carry the phone with him, keeping his left hand on the hardness. The phone cord snaking around the corner behind him seemed to writhe with the tension. He felt its approval as he placed the phone down next to him on the narrow bed; he would be careful not to push it off the edge. He lay close to the wall, on his back, both hands covering the front of his pants. He must prepare a picture in his mind, women in various positions—no, not today. No voices, either. His crotch gave a deeper throb, he'd have to hurry now. Yes, yes, the black rubbered cord, wound around his ankles, over and around, he was bound there, helpless, someone slowly unbuckled his belt, he could not stop, someone zipped down his pants, the buzz of a hungry, lazy sound in his dream. He was helpless, the cord held him still, the telephone a spectator; he closed his eyes tight and sank into the hands. He felt the room drift away; he no longer swam, he no longer stroked the deep waters, but floating just beneath the surface, he let go. Held only by the two hands gripping him and the cord around his feet, down and down.

He opened his eyes and reached for the phone. His finger sought the hole of the first number.

The Dead of July

I go all day wearing Mama's face. I feel it sliding over mine in that tight rubber-glove way as I drive to work. I know it the instant I finish talking to someone I haven't met before, but disapprove of . . . not because of anything they've done or said, but just because. Mama always disapproved of something about almost everyone.

This is the way the face looks: the skin pulls over your bones like thin rubber stretched tight—the rubber glove. It's that way so the mouth can't do anything drastic, like smile. It can only get thin as paper. And with some effort, the corners pull in and down. That's what Mama got from her mother—that's the Methodist in them. And the eyes, well, they're blank, neutral as flour. And the brow, it pulls up a little, into the scalp, so it would look surprised if the eyes had any light in them. But all you get is the Methodist again.

Well, this is the story of the dead of July—the air so still you hate to disturb it breathing. The cat runs off. She's had enough to last a lifetime of my kicking covers off and pulling them back on. The fan's noisy rattle runs my sleep from midnight to dawn, then light breaks through and captures the room anyway. The fan seems useless against the heat crouched outside the front door. I get up to let it in.

Overhead the noisy growl of approaching planes, and outside the stillness of things too hot to move or grow. This is how we reach into August, and later September, but for now, it seems impossible that anything will change again. This is the middle of July.

In the paper the accidents start. The boy and his girl turn mad as dogs, running loose through the middle states, killing and stealing, not paying much attention to which they do. And a nun from two towns over hangs herself in the attic of our old Catholic church. Just visiting her folks. We knew something was up when the bell started ringing on a Tuesday. But it was too late. Cancer. Despair. We all know enough, even the Methodists, to understand how bad it is with her—cast down to hell and shame. Her family walking around like they're embarrassed to shop at the A&P anymore. I can understand their worry. Now I feel mama's face glitter like clear nail polish when I see them on the street.

This is a mean time. Birds squabbling in the bush outside the trailer, rising like cinders and burnt scraps of paper from a fire, tossing above the trees then dropping back. In the morning, all they've got in them is a couple of chirps before the sun gets up good, then it's back to sitting where it's cool.

Lazy. That's what Mama's face says. Lazy as dogs. The cat didn't run off, she'd tell me, it got tired of having to work. Left a drift of black fur on the counter with its dirty paw prints and took off. Good riddance, Mama's face says.

But I don't listen to this face all the time, after all, she said that when Jake took off, too. Methodists like to keep things neat, I have to remind myself. Especially the old kind. They don't hold with things that can get sloppy on you—dancing, playing cards, smoking and drinking.

Especially drinking. You should've seen Mama's face the day Jake brought home his first case of beer and stacked it neatly, all of it, in twelve-ounce cans, in the bottom of the fridge. Like we were taking a trip to the moon and he was stocking provisions.

There is a lot that makes me wear that face in the middle of July though. This is the face I wear for the summer heat, for the disapproval that lets me sleep alone.

Yesterday I was at the laundromat. No place hotter in July, the clothes thumping hot against the hot dryer walls, when you pull them out, they grab hold of you like they're going to keep thumping. I come out needing a bath after every weekly trip. Anyway, I heard these ladies talking about the nun—said she'd had cancer in her face, it'd eaten her sinuses away so she couldn't bear the weather. The worst thing was to get a cold and have to sneeze, like acid was being run through her head. Then it went for her eyes. She started trying all these cures—positive thinking, natural foods, she even went to Texas, where some guy claimed he could arrest your cancer with marigold pollen. It made her allergic. She came home puffed up like a pumpkin and had to take drugs and eat out of a straw for the rest of her time. Finally it got so bad that she was seeing double all the time, and every little sound rang in her head so loud she couldn't think straight. Like the cancer'd made a clear channel in there, like a sea shell, and she couldn't take the roar of the ocean anymore.

They figure she was only praying at first, but it must've been pretty tempting to climb the stairs to the old bell tower. Her head as round and carved as metal by the time the cancer was through, just her brain hanging there like an oyster surprised when the blade slits open the shell. I maintain that that's July for you. When nothing seems to grow and you begin to believe you'll never get cool again. Never sleep a whole night again. Never have your own face back.

July. This is the time when you try to keep things the way they always are. You know better than to introduce a change, like putting different horses together in a pasture. The kicks connect in July, they break jaws and legs. Horses down, horses rolling in pain, horses on three legs, that's July.

When I dream, it's of big, too big houses, wrapped in white cotton and it's getting cold out. All through the dream the temperature drops like someone's sucking at it from outside the picture, and when I go to sleep, the blanket's too thin and worn to keep me warm. But all that space, I figure I can make it through the winter.

I suppose it would be the normal thing for the divorce rate to go up then, for people to turn tail and head for Nebraska, Missouri, ports east, but that's not usual. When the weather turns on us, we like the comfort of someone to fight with, someone to be the soft connector to the arm, the fist slashed out, the anger bubbling under the skin that's cooking in the heat. No, they leave later when the heat breaks, when it looks like a chance for a fresh start, not now, when there's nowhere to go anyway, when the physical effort of having emotions is too much. When the indifference makes falling into bed with someone an act of infidelity, even if you're married to them.

That's probably why I ended up sleeping with Jerry. It was probably easier than going home to my own bed with Jake. I just couldn't face the drive in that heat.

I don't even think I bothered taking Mama's face off before he was on top of me. It wouldn't have mattered. I was too hot to be disapproving, even of myself. All I remember is the suck of our chests together, a sound like something breathing in that nun's head, and his hands rolling my nipples like they were balls of beer-soaked napkin on the table back at Sleepy's, where we'd been drinking. His hair and skin weren't any worse than mine, soaked in smoke and beer and dull conversation, floating on the green breath of July heat.

Later, we lay panting side by side, trying not to touch, in the wet sheets, while the sun finally plopped down like a fat lady on a couch and fell backwards over the hill. The mosquito almost too lazy to strike, walked deliberately up my arm and with the precision of a surgeon began to sting. I had to debate whether it was worth the effort to slap it.

What She Knew

The sound of the dog creaking down the stairs stopped midflight as he evidently paused to look out the small knee-high rectangle of leaded glass—the world beyond, gray with rain and dirty snow piled along the street edge, must have seemed good to him. She heard the dog sigh and resume down the stairs, the exact moment of his entrance into the hallway marked by the distinct tap of each claw on the wood floor. He walked past her and into the living room beyond, not even stopping to sniff the knee of her jeans. He circled the living room once and returned to the hallway—again ignoring her at the table. As he settled into an awkward clump on the floor, facing the stair down to the front door, he gave a slight sound, not quite a whine or cry—maybe he had to go to the bathroom, she thought. Oh, well. He'd been trained to wait until night. To hold it in.

She couldn't find a clock anywhere in the house. Walking from room to room, she thought how strange not to know what time. The light fading from the windows. The dog's bladder was filling like a sack of water—the kind of canvas bag she'd seen hanging off the front grills of cars coming through the desert. His crotch must ache by now, the walking and lying down only jarring it against the skeleton. A sweet pain.

Her breasts swollen hard with milk—for once, she had *needed* a bra to carry each one in its sling. Milk had oozed from the nipples, which seemed erect and tender forever. She had longed for them to be sucked—to be drained— they had ached with the weight of the fluid. She had wanted to taste it but was always afraid. She had wanted her husband to drink it, but would not allow him. She had forced herself to save it all for the child, felt guilty when once she had milked the engorged breasts—leaning naked over the tub in the tiny bathroom, the backs of her legs nearly touching the coldsweated toilet—when no one was around, to avoid the stains on her blouse, to relieve the pressure just once. She had watched the pale liquid stream from her body onto the rust-stained porcelain, form rivulets to the drain and then disappear.

She inspected the lines on her palm as he made his proposal over the phone—they were changing again. A cross below her index finger, head line plunging into palm more deeply. "Are you there?" his voice interrupted. "I don't quite know how to say this . . . I mean . . . I made a list of the girls I knew and you were the first. I have to ask you, I have to do it now—I want to sleep with you. I know this is strange, but you understand I couldn't ask anyone else." She felt calm.

Surprise edged with pride and insult. She was sitting in the doorway of the kitchen, her legs and feet tucked tightly under her—she felt chilled. Did he know? How could he know. Only Paul. He didn't know anyone. Maybe people knew then—they looked and knew. Handprints of it on her face and arms.

A drop of spaghetti sauce dotted her blouse. She tried to wash it but couldn't—then it didn't matter. When he picked her up, she showed him the stain.

"Here, sit down while I get the stuff." She watched him slide down the embankment to the car parked below. The unused roads above and around them made her imagine 3 A.M.

"OK. I got it all. This jar is your whiskey—I snuck some of my father's. Here is a glass. Sorry it's warm. It's all I could find." He handed her the glass. She began to sip at it, burning her throat to cough.

"This is the rubber which I'll leave right here next to the blanket. Are you comfortable? I thought of a pillow, but didn't bring it. How's the whiskey?"

She nodded and watched him straighten the blanket on the ledge, which was actually wide enough for them both to sit or lie down side by side. He's methodical, she thought. Under his mind he's making lists. Careful, careful, careful.

They listened to distant cars sounding in the night. Some birds. His arm around her. Warm. Kissing. Hugging. Hand leg. Shorts. She was wearing shorts. Yes, a bra. Oh, do I unhook now? Please. This and this. This. Darkkiss tongue. Later. I put it on. This way. Do you want to touch it? Do you want to touchit. Do you? Do you? Sitting. I read about. You. Have you ever, woulddidcould? We. Please. Yes.

The room was growing colder. Everywhere snow. She listened but the dog was quiet. A wind came up outside. She had sealed the windows so the curtains didn't blow anymore. Sunlight through the three windows shadowed her hands across the paper. She wrote deliberately.

She turned to the man. To the stranger. Her bed, its white iron rods trimmed in brass. Now, a stranger also. The lace walls covered another mystery. This man. This man began to swim her body a river. Her blood a current. He swam up and up with the flow of water. She tossed her liquid form against his sure one. And he dove hard, chasing a fish—the fish silvery in the darkness and broad and flat. A man swimming a woman. Stroking from side to side, the ballet twist of water weaving the rocks into itself. Of fish threading its soul onto the current. Up and up, the man swam toward the river's mouth and the dark skyspace he knew beyond. That fish would burst a star new into blackness. She pulled him into her—her body a swift river led him on. And on. Until the blood broke between them and he lay shivering on his side in the calm deep waters. Inside her. She, with the fishman, stared into the blackshadow room. Not. Not. Not. A whisper.

Enough streetlight from the uncurtained top of the window to outline the head of the actress leaving the Moulin Rouge. Even Lautrec's stumpy figure walks the other way. Her blue gown moving in a speckled yellow nest of day. The oil lamp on her desk leaned slightly to the left, the flashlight next to it appeared in contrast to favor the right. She had to tell herself over and over it was simply an illusion.

Figures outlined themselves in her mind. She even noticed their movements along the carpet. Corner dwellers. Her own hair caught in peripheral sight, joined the others. Slowly. She watched the world of hardness, those forms formal to themselves, pull away from her. She expected a list of demands very soon. Conditions of release.

Getting up from her chair, she calls the dog to her. His obedience. Here, here, here. They walk side by side into the living room, her hand resting slightly on his head, almost the height of her hip. She lays down on the rug. Had not turned on the light in late afternoon dark. He watches, standing near her head. She looks for the signal in his eyes—deeper into his skull, back to where the buried animal lives. He moves closer. Feeds herself into his eyes.

The room gets darker—it is, after all, winter. Outside the sound of cars bearing people home from work slowly fades.

After the Movies

After the Sunday afternoon movies, my brother Tolson and I are walking home, half running and half walking, taunting each other. We are young. We must not be over ten or eleven—that is, me—because my brother, who isn't my twin, couldn't be the same age, and we always acted like we were until that night we had the fight and hit each other in the crotch with a new understanding that that was where it hurt, and from then on we were different ages forever.

It was winter, and there was that thin, runny sunshine that made everything look like it just woke up or something out there. But there was probably a dull sparkle, because I remember it white with snow and gray with ice, and that would be right, too—it being winter and Iowa and all. Folks don't realize how cold it can get here, and how much snow. Or maybe they do, but they think up north is the real place for hard winters, and I guess I can't argue with that any. I spent a couple of them up there with Jake when we first got together, and then I said, no sir, I'm going south, which was Iowa, and not south at all to lots of folks—but to Minnesota it's south. So it's sort of relative, I figure, like the way the sun shone that day, which was not that bright January light.

But this day—and I'm pretty sure of this because it's the way I see it when it all comes back to me, although I haven't told Jake any of this. He's not much interested in the past, he claims, and snuggles up real close, so how can I disagree with that? And I don't mean to, let me tell you. That's why we get along so good, much to the surprise of everyone in his family—but that's another story, and I was going to tell you this thing that happened.

So my brother and I are skipping along and decide to take the shortcut across the ruined amusement park. All the rides are gone—just some trees and dirt with a bit of grass thrown in once in a while—but it lets us out of an extra block, and that was good sense. Even after this, we always did that, though I must say I felt considerably different about the shortcut later. There were some older boys playing hockey on the little flooded ice pond there. The town was good that way, coming out to the parks with their water trucks or turning on the fire hydrants if they were handy, just for the sake of the kids, and we'd watch the water freeze first with a skin like the top of boiled milk, nothing anyone with sense would put a foot on, though sometimes one of the neighbor kids would try, or throw a stick through, and that was dumb because if the weather held, we'd have to skate and slide around that stick all winter then. And the kid would have to be embarrassed each time he took a look at it. But being the kind of kids we were, probably none of them were embarrassed at all, and just forgot that it was them threw the stick in whcn it started to freeze up good, and went along complaining to beat the band like the rest at the interruption. But most of us waited while the city came out each freezing day and pumped another layer of water onto the spot.

It was lovely at night after they did that. The little pond looked almost like enamel, clean and undented. You knew if you went down there, alone, with just the dim streetlight over your head, that you'd still see some reflection of yourself coming back *dark* at you, like you were buried in there, under that frozen water, and come spring, they'd all be surprised to see you again, and wouldn't the neighborhood buzz with that. But I never went there like that, only to skate sometimes, to practice the spins I learned in lessons my Girl Scout troop took. The leaders never knew what to do with us. They always had us going to one thing or another, and little treats at the end of each weekly meeting, hoping they could hold it together until we went to high school and lost interest. They just wanted to get to that stage, and I don't blame them; I learned a lot of things halfway because of them, and I suppose for that I should be thankful. Couldn't ever skate backwards, but Jake says it don't matter, long as you skate good frontways. He's that way—understanding. Besides, he likes to watch that little skirt I put on when I'm skating. Still wear the one I made in high school so many years ago. I'm proud of that, not many can stay like I have.

But I was telling you what happened that day. See, it was late afternoon, about four, just before the sun was going to go plunk, and we knew we'd finish the walk home in the dark and we didn't much like the thin winter dark. It wasn't friendly the way it was in summer, when everything is still noisy-awake regardless of night, and the air, being so warm, just sort of holds onto you. This winter time was unfriendly as all get-out, and we told each other stories about the children who had frozen to death in the snow, stories we'd grown up on, I suppose, to make us afraid of winter so we'd stay around home, or just curiosities, maybe that was all it was. Maybe parents never thought anything, just opened their mouths and out came this stuff that scared all hell out of us.

But I remember that that must have been part of why we took the shortcut, too. We wanted to get closer to home when the sun went down, and so we started across

the park and the boys playing hockey—they were big
boys, I know that. Know that I saw that right away, but
we weren't afraid of them necessarily. We were minding
our own business. We were just skipping along, and all
of a sudden this big redheaded one steps in front of me—
which was surprising because I wasn't on the lookout for
that sort of move—and I stop, and my brother he stops
a few yards ahead of me. We're all just standing around
then, and the other boys have paused there in their game,
and they're watching what's happening, but I can't
remember them at all, a single face, what anyone was
wearing—so it must not have been anything.

And this redhead starts asking me my name, and I tell
him sort of quiet and shy. I don't know this boy and it's
dawning on me to be a little uncomfortable. What would
he want to know me for? He wasn't a friend of my older
sister or brother, I was pretty sure of that. My brother is
up there ahead, just watching, he doesn't do a thing,
doesn't take a step toward me. And this boy starts in teas-
ing me, saying words I don't understand, like he wants
something, and I get the feeling that I shouldn't be standing beside this ice pond talking to a "stranger" like this,
but he's not a strange man in a car, I tell myself. He's not
unwrapping himself the way that man did to Marion, and
she was the prettiest girl we knew. Men followed her in
cars home from school. She always had bad things happening like that, and we all respected her for the hard time
she had of it, being pretty and all, and we sort of understood that life wasn't going to be easy for someone like
Marion.

But this boy wasn't a strange man in a car and there
was the confusion. He was an older boy and he wasn't
doing anything and then he was. He was asking me if I
wanted to _____ and he said a word I didn't know
what it meant, never heard or seen the word, not even
painted on the outside of the high school stadium walls,

where boys wrote curses and things about wild girls they knew. No one ever used that word then, so it was the first time and you can't blame me. I just stood there looking at my brother who was ignoring me now, scraping his foot along a snowy place, digging up the dead leaves and twigs and trash like that. I wanted to tell him, "stop that, you're making a mess." But this redheaded boy was stepping closer, and I knew the sun was starting to drop because it got real sharp and orange over the houses to our right and this boy cupped his hand up to me then, pushing my jeans in right between my legs. "Want to?" he whispered now, so no one but us two could hear. "Want to ____?" and he said the word again. I couldn't move, and my brother was looking toward home with something like longing, it seems now, and the other boys were statues off to our left, and the sun kept going down as fast as it could and nothing was going to stop this, and his fingers made me warm like water up there, and suddenly I *knew* it was wrong. And when he whispered again, bent down so close to me, his red hair like a sun burning the top of his head off, I knew the answer and shook my head. No, I whispered back, then, NO, louder, and ran around him as quick as I could, running hard past my brother who picked up the chase, running as fast as that sun, running before that boy could stop me and get back the fingers I could feel left between my legs.

I wanted to tell my brother then, about that warmth that made the winter go away for a while, but instead I ran harder and he ran harder. We were racing, and by the time we turned the corner of the grade school we attended, five blocks from home, we were both falling down out of breath. As soon as we could talk, I warned him, "Don't you tell, don't you dare tell them," and he nodded agreement and I knew he wouldn't. I knew somehow that he would get in trouble, too. But I always hated him a little bit after that for the secret he knew, for the hand he saw between my legs when he looked at me. And I did take it out on him. And he seems to feel the same. Now, after I told all this, I think maybe Jake is right, it doesn't do any good at all to talk about the past, does it?

The Story of the Belt

Thereere was the one his mother hung around her neck. Don't get it wrong—she wasn't any martyr to the household. When the dishes weren't done and papers clung to the carpet like puddles of snow, this one whacked the bottoms and legs till silence reigned. With smoke curling around her face from the cigarette perched between her lips, the small faces looked up and saw God, saw a volcano, saw the red coal of hate in her mouth and fell down before that biting belt.

You'd like to say that the belt got tied around his arm later, got pulled tight between the teeth so there were permanent bite marks after that, like some mad insect at work, but that wouldn't be true. There wasn't even the romance of self-destruction in him. He hid the belt and avoided drugs.

His brother found alcohol easier to come by, more suitable for an ethnic statement. Drunk, he won the track meets, drunk, he won the prizes, passed the tests, dated the girls, raped his sister. At least his brother had an excuse. That's what they were to say later among themselves. Where's the belt?

Don't worry. That wasn't much of a problem for him. His brother was made a coward though, and couldn't stop ruining himself after that. His brother asked for it. Ask anyone.

The belt sprang to life, Lazarus of Punishment, even after he'd hidden it. It reappeared being pulled with a whispery whish from the loops of Father's pants at dinnertime each night. "Your son has been driving me crazy." In the rules listed on the back of the door, just above checkout time, someone should have read to his brother: don't bother Mom.

The beatings were regular, therapeutic, took the tension out of them both. Brother curled into a baby ball in the corner of his bed, believing that his cries would stop the belt above him, which he watched at first in slow motion, rising like a scarf in the wind, then settling down on him, its silky touch that ended in sting. Then the picture sped up and the hurt began, so he stopped watching and felt only the hand of the belt, an inch and a half wide as it identified his body to him. This was the way he got to know himself: elbows and stomach, thighs and buttocks, shoulders and ankles—the strap made them friends. Then enemies. It sealed his skin like Saran Wrap and shoved him into the fridge like leftovers no one was interested in. Brother felt himself rotting inside, felt the skin get so numb, nothing could get out, get in. He wished for something like a knife—it wasn't an easy job.

He, on the other hand, was the good one who went away to school and came home. He babysat, dreamy as a girl, while upstairs, his brother tore the clothes off their eight-year-old sister.

This belt began its magic early in the family, appearing and disappearing like a household god. When the brothers grew up, one refused to wear a belt. Can you guess which? One bought a belt with two tongues, double buckling. Embossed with a clever basket weave, brass, it was almost too ornate to wear. But he did anyway. He was the one who hid. He was the one who forgot. He was the one who didn't know. He never knew. Later, the others would accuse him: you never cared. But he'd known enough to protect them by hiding the belt, he wanted to say, but couldn't think of it, the words.

Now he lives in a house that heaves up the middle, everything runs away from the center, furniture tilts, water slides away from a split like a mountain stream. There's an earthquake so far down below the surface, the basement. Somewhere so deep, the giant back of the snake humps and writhes, the house on its back jiggles and cracks with the strain. Someday, the concrete will burst, the crack become a chasm, the skin of stucco will shed, the rooms sloughed in a tangle, a pale outline of dark and light. There will be something to say then, won't there?

Young

And at twilight, as car lights bend the night into its coming, in twilight in spring, when moisture is thick in our noses and skins, when we are almost burdened with the threat of vegetation in the air, in that early evening which turns the nearby streets lavender and gray and rose, the car lights beckoning home, blindly, with the instincts of night creatures driving back and back, then in twilight they begin, one here and one there, slowly they gather, perch on the shoulder-high fences that cut off one yard from another, contain the dogs we need, then in spring they find each other like migratory birds, with swanning chests, tipped here and there by color, they group, as if secreted by the houses, an accretion of time, they find each other as surely as their age, blindly, with the instinct of that warm small chirring body of bird that it is time to move -an ache in the mouth, the unused muscles of their lives—they seek and find each other, recognize, know—with the sureness of animals, their own kind—sometimes there is a movement, shifting of tension from one leg to the next, hands thrust in pockets, heads up and down with the constant pecking of here and there, to get a better look at the nothing they concentrate on, and it is always spring and evening when they smell it, each other, through the dense new air.

We see them clustering along the fences, talking quietly for hours, only their faces glow through the darkness, we see their liquid grouping, the containment, the pressure of their presence threatening to overflow at any moment, but they are silent, they are silent, smelling, nosing each other, waiting for direction like birds hunched before rain, they exchange some knowledge of the place and wait for time to go faster.

Today

Around me the house, the people, the animals make decisions. The toaster produces the amount of brownness it considers right. I can't get it browner, burned almost, as I like it. No matter how many times I punch it back it returns just as quickly. It makes these decisions. I am not certain that they are made in my interest. I suspect that I have little to do with it. No reason to think so. I don't want to anthropomorphize or anything—that could be foolish, assuming that the toaster oven in the corner under the cabinet to the right of the sink cared about me.

I go upstairs and prepare to type, turn on the heater in my little room, hoping that the dust that has settled into its coils all summer does not come whooshing out and activate my allergy—not intentionally, you understand. I don't think that the heater holds a kind of malevolence in its metal-brown grid. Then I scoot into my adjacent bedroom for some thick socks, since this add-on part of the house is always cold. My neck is sore—I can barely hold it up—from the Indian leg wrestling I did last night with someone a hundred pounds heavier and eight inches taller. I thought I could win. In fact, I could not believe that I could not win. Now it's more doctor bills and silly explanations, but I had a choice, I understand that—break my neck or not, and what's interesting is that I kept repeating the defeat, biting hard on my tongue each time.

When I come back into the little room prepared now for the work ahead, I see that my stool is not in its customary place in front of the typewriter. That means that it is serving alternative duty as a TV holder in my daughter's room. I turn around twice on my way in there. I would like to say that I thought about it like that, that something told me to wait, maybe I could sit on something else to type, maybe I could wait to type, but then I just wanted the stool. She would be asleep, after all. As I open the door, I don't even glance at the bed, so certain am I that she is asleep, and like the way I used to enter my older sister's room—the one who slept all the time in a nest of her anger and dislike for me. I always tried to pretend that I wasn't there, that I wasn't going to her closet to get something. I mean I always thought that maybe I could get away with it like that, that somehow she wouldn't notice as I pulled the little closet light on so it shone on her bed and face, because what I wanted to avoid was that voice that came through me like a knife, that pierced all of my intentions, good and bad, with the clarity of its utter disdain.

So I didn't glance at the bed at first, but the scurry, the sudden movements, not even a cry, a sound but louder than that, made me look, and there they were—my daughter's face like an animal's, hollow with surprise and fear.

Again I turn around to leave but realize that now, more than ever, I need the stool, and foolishly I turn again, ignoring the stereo rock softly orchestrating the room's behavior, the flickering candle. "But it's morning," I want to say, and reach out for it. I have this sudden urge to tidy the room, to go downstairs for a giant green plastic garbage bag, to throw all the things around me into it, the bottles and the cigarette butts, the plates of dried food, the records and the stereo, the candle—oh, it's old and useless enough—and I could make the bed up and put them back to sleep, put them back into it, cleanly, without this mess.

But I don't touch anything. I lift the too-heavy TV, and then suddenly there is nowhere to put it. As I try to set it gently on the floor, I am aware that a large brown tennis shoe is obstructing its balance. I push at it halfheartedly with my foot, but can't budge it on the thick carpet. The rubber sole is too adhesive and I give up, placing the TV at some drunken angle on the spine of the shoe, thinking only now as an afterthought that it might ruin the shoe's conformation, and after all, they weren't that old. Then I glance over again to the bed, only then, and only to the bottom next to me. I am close enough to lean over and touch it, and the covers have pulled up and away now, a tangle of feet there, remarkable feet I think, those thin boyish legs kids that age share in common, and his larger feet some promise of later, and her's smaller and what they will be forever, and around his ankles, in a hurry, his underwear, and this somehow saddens me—and no, I am not angry.

"Get dressed," I say, "and we'll talk." But I don't mean it, as I pick up the stool and stumble apologetically from the room, remembering to close the door just as she likes, quietly and firmly.

What the Fall Brings

The fall here in Divinity, Iowa, always brings back such memories that I almost go running home with a sack over my head so I don't have to watch them come ghosting up high over the buildings, or leaking out of doorways like someone's washer running crazy and crazy.

Some days, I feel my body with my own hands, you know, just to make sure I'm here and not evaporating like some of the people I've known. But I've seen the way bones break, and the way they resist and grow back, so I figure they can stand a lot. I also figure that maybe they aren't so different—the folks around here—from anyplace else. I mean, we got a certain number that end up in Anamosa, the state penitentiary, not much more or less than anywhere else. We got the same regular numbers being trucked over to Independence (the mental hospital's there) by their families, or occasionally by the deputy, the squad car light whirring most of the way, just to impress everyone with the importance of his errand. And yearly, the same number more or less heads on out to the cemetery, usually carried along in the big black hearse belonging to Thompson's Mortuary, but occasionally arriving from out of town in someone else's. We get used to it. All our friends and family are there after a while.

I like to think about all of us years from now, where we'll be, how many of us will still be going to the same jobs, the same daily routines, say, twenty or thirty years from now. Since I'm just turning thirty now, hell, I could live to be a hundred, but I don't think many others will. It might be awfully lonely then. I might end up like Miss Ethel's mother—all bones and a bag of skin. What I'm afraid of, is that maybe as you get older, things start falling out of place. Maybe a rib could detach, maybe your shoulder blades could start traveling around. It's a funny idea, I know, but after the way I've watched things start to loosen in people, it's something to think about.

Like every fall, I can't help thinking about that one time after the state fair, just when everything was beginning to color up nice, early October. I was still in high school, just my first year, I think—yes, that'd be right, because that's how I still knew him. We'd gone through grade school once I'd moved up here, and he was the second boy I kissed. The first one didn't work, so it took me a long time to work up nerve again. But Billy Bond was sure a lot nicer about it. We were in seventh grade. Billy lived on a farm outside of town, and although the school bus took him back and forth, often as not he'd walk me home, then go on and walk all the way, five miles out, just so he'd be able to spend a little more time with me. I know his daddy must have given it to him for always being late for chores, but Billy worked pretty hard, so no one could complain too much. Everyone in my family just pretended like Billy Bond wasn't there—that was their way usually. And I do recall that in the next year, the eighth grade, when Billy decided to like LuAnn Menderson instead of me, it did come as a blow. But then, LuAnn lived on the farm next to his, and I guess they could take the bus home together and see each other more, so it made sense, sort of. Better sense than walking five miles just to see me.

And they were both in 4H, I remember that. It's a big deal for kids out here, 4H and Future Farmers of America when they got a little older. They'd all walk around in their shiny satin jackets with the fancy stitching along over the front pocket—their nicknames—and in the back, the big round symbol and title—Future Farmers of America. It was like a fraternity. When they went to college, they studied agriculture and animal husbandry and came home and took over the farms, going through the usual fights with dads and older relatives about new ideas the ag school was pumping out in its monthly bulletins. Like how many cows a man without a hired help could maintain efficiently versus the farmer with help. And whether the hay was better baled and stacked, rolled in giant rounds and left in the field, or racked into long cylinders like old-fashioned curls and then bound with twine and put up in the barn. Every farmer had his pet theories, and every farmer fought with his kids from ag school about the changes.

I know, because you used to have to listen to it everywhere you went. In school the boys would get into fistfights about whose dad knew the most, and whether you want China blacks or Polands in hogs, and which wintered best—the shelled corn or the unshelled. And there was a hierarchy, too, depending on what you raised—cattle at the top, hogs in the middle and poultry at the bottom. Billy explained it once when we went to the county fair. We spent most of the day in the animal 4H exhibits, while I just wanted to ride the ferris wheel and have Billy win me a big panda bear. But Billy was a serious person; he had a big stake in doing a good job with his pig growing and didn't want to mess up by letting anything go. So we spent most of the time checking on this big old mama hog, fat as a piece of butter and smelling pretty good, with just the hint of piggy odor about her. Billy told me that he used Wella Balsam Creme Rinse on her hair to get it to lie flat and smell good. He liked the piney smell of it. Then he made me put my face down into the pen, with my nose almost touching her pink skin. He was right—piney, with just an edge of hog underneath.

God, the things he showed me to do to a pig. He'd stolen some of his mama's clear fingernail polish, and after rasping his hog's little hoofs rounded and smooth, he painted them up with the polish. Boy, did they shine. Since the animals were kept bedded in clean, sweet straw, they didn't have a chance to go out and act like pigs, get dirty again. It was like an animal palace at those fairs, the animals just lounging around, nothing to do but lie there or stand and have some person spend hours picking their ears or getting every last crumb out of their coat. Why, if you forgot these were farm animals, you'd think you were at one of those dog-grooming parlors watching fancy little poodles getting bows put in their hair or something. When I tried a joke with Billy, asking him why he'd neglected putting some eye make-up on his pig, he gave me a strange look, reddened, then opened his trunk sitting just outside the pen, and pulled out some Maybelline eyeliner and mascara. "I thought about it . . . ." I didn't have the heart to laugh, so I just nodded serious-like and let it go.

I don't want you to get me wrong here though, Billy Bond wasn't the only one. These kids ate, slept, dreamed their animals. There wasn't a one of them wouldn't do what Billy was doing. It was a strange sight, believe me, to look down the rows and rows of those 4H barns and see kids with their animals, some of them sleeping in the stall, some of them outside it. Some of them bent over as they handpicked each particle of manure out, and some of them looking like little mamas, dressing their babies with a tenderness and consideration that only comes from a genuine love.

I suppose that if Billy hadn't been so careful, so meticulous about his hog raising—if he'd let something slip by, if he'd gotten interested in girls more, or horsing around with his friends when he should have been handfeeding and grooming—then things would have turned out different in the long run. But you don't get anywhere thinking like that, I guess. The facts are what they are. Like bones— there one day, and then who knows, maybe it's the skin that lets go of them somehow.

But I remember that the fall of our freshman year in high school, Billy Bond's hog, Bluebell, won the grand championship at the Iowa State Fair. She was the biggest and the best. There were pictures of Billy and his hog in newspapers all over Iowa. They were a winning couple, and besides, the pig was the biggest ever to win the 4H, and you knew that that was going to set Billy up for good as a hog grower. People remembered those things, and if Billy's pigs could turn that size and quality, then Billy wouldn't have a thing to worry about. Everyone was proud of him, I recall, his dad and brothers strutting around town like they were behind the whole thing. There was even a little parade the day Billy and Bluebell came home when the fair was done. They drove real slow down Main Street, and the high school band played some snappy songs, and the hog looked out the grates of the little trailer, sniffing suspiciously like she knew just what was going to happen next.

Because it was part of it that Bluebell had been auctioned and bought by Reese's A&P and would spend a couple of weeks on display for everyone to see right in front of the store, to honor Billy and the pig and the 4H. Half the proceeds were to go to the club in town, to build future 4Hers like Billy, and Reese could take the tax write-off and sell or donate the meat as the highest grade pork around. But Billy looked pretty miserable through the whole thing, even while he was squatting down, posing with his arm thrown around Bluebell's shoulder for the newspaper photographs. And I remember how when the picture came out a few days later, it reminded me of a boy and his girl watching a movie, the same intent distracted look on each of their faces.

I've never much liked to see animals on display, like at zoos, or at fairs and carnivals, and I think Billy's hog just reinforced that for me. It was sad to walk by her every time you wanted to get a loaf of bread at the A&P. Bluebell always came trotting up to the little portable fence, sniffing like you'd brought it a treat, like Billy probably taught it to do, then when you didn't haven anything for it, she would shuffle back to the far corner and stand with her back to you, dejected. And while their mamas shopped the little kids were spending too much time tormenting her, throwing little rocks and clods of dirt to watch her stampede around, then they'd have a laughing fit seeing all that wobbly fat. I think it'd been Reese's idea to build some publicity for the hog slaughter, and put even more fat on her by keeping her confined and stuffing her good for a couple of weeks. I don't think he intended more than that. Reese is pretty harmless. He just wants to make his money and let it go at that.

Every afternoon after school, those two weeks, Billy Bond would come over, snap a little collar and lead line on the pig and take it out back to the vacant lot to eat grass and get some exercise. He was careful, though, not to let her run much since they wanted to keep the fat on and Reese had warned him about it. And I swear, the time or two I caught sight of it, Billy and that hog looked just like a boy romping with his dog at a distance.

In Divinity, the homecoming game on Saturday afternoon is the biggest celebration of the fall, and since we knew we'd win that year, everyone was real built up. You could feel it all week as you walked down the street, in and out of stores, people a bit more pumped up than usual, joshing the football players they saw, or the families of the players. As part of the celebration afterwards, Reese had decided to butcher the hog and have a big pig roast. To help things along, some of the merchants had gotten together and decided to buy a couple of kegs of beer for the adults and pop for the kids. So all morning before the game that started at one in the afternoon, the A&P had been busy with folks coming and going, buying food to fix and taking things down to the little park beside the river a couple of blocks away. The hardware store had donated some strings of lights and the men were busy with those, putting them into the trees overhead, setting up tables and chairs and cleaning up the little bandstand.

I don't think anyone thought much about the empty pen outside the store. People were used to the animals that came and went from season to season. Farm kids learned early that that was the way things were. I guess I didn't keep track either. It was the first high school homecoming I was actually going to be a part of, like I belonged instead of some dumb kid running around. And I had a date, my first, although I had to take my sister Baby along, so nothing could happen. Kenton Maxwell, the boy, told me not to worry though, he was a year older than me and knew how to get around big obstacles like Baby. Just before one that afternoon, we'd walked up to the game, the three of us from my house, where Kenton's brother had let him out. None of us but Baby were old enough to drive yet, and Baby was too big to fit behind a normal steering wheel, so she still couldn't. EuGene, as usual, wouldn't have a thing to do with any of us, and just drove off in his empty car to pick up his date. I was so excited, I guess I didn't think much about the aroma of roasting pig that drifted through that afternoon, it was all part of the excitement—the game, the picnic and dance later. And I was going to all of it. Probably no one even missed Billy Bond, not even his family, because everything was focused on his brothers, who were on the varsity string playing that afternoon.

Of course, our small towns always choose to play the smallest, weakest team they can find for their homecoming, and I don't know who this team could play since it came from such a small community that they were barely fielding the two lines. To no one's surprise, we trounced them good and sent them brokenhearted and brokenheaded onto their buses at four, for the long ride back home, while we all came busting out of the field, running for our cars and the victory parade down Main Street afterwards.

Some of the high school clubs had fixed up floats, and the candidates for homecoming queen were all dressed up, sitting on the backs of honking convertibles. It was the sort of thing that is still going on each October in this town. But the reason I remember this one so well is Billy Bond, who had climbed on top of the four-story bank building, the tallest we have, right in the center of town while everyone was at the game, and who was, apparently, driven crazy by the sight and smell of the beloved Bluebell turning slowly over the coals in the late afternoon sun, because by the time the parade was half way through town, he had picked up the BB gun he'd climbed up to the roof with and started shooting at things in the street below him, hollering.

I can still remember how loud his voice was. You could hear it clearly, plainly, above the marching band even. Although the range was too much for the BB gun most of the time, he managed to pop one under the skin of Reese's forearm before everyone took cover. Reese was plenty mad when that happened, and after a moment of shock, then realization that it was Billy Bond up on the bank roof taking pot shots and messing up the parade, he sneaked into the drugstore and called the sheriff's office, which was stupid, since the sheriff and his deputy were both on their posse quarter horses leading the parade like always. When Reese realized this, he went ducking and sneaking down the street to where the two men sat on their horses, taking stock of the situation, well out of range of the BB gun.

Reese demanded that they do something, "take the little bugger off of there," calling Billy every name in the book and waving his forearm with the welt from the BB rising red and angry, looking like a big spider had bit him or something. The sheriff was trying hard to hold off a smile—you could see that a mile away—and whether Reese could or not, I don't know, but he could sure tell he wasn't getting anywhere, because in a few minutes he stomped his feet and started walking straight back to his place in the parade, forgetting about Billy for a moment until a BB ticked the top of his head, ruffling the hair enough to send him cursing and sliding into the cover of the hardware store. Then he started yelling right up at Billy, saying, "Goddamn you, Billy Bond, I'm gonna get you for this. You're going to Anamosa, you goddamn juvenile delinquent," and stuff like this. Billy just answered by showering the street below with more BBs—he had a Daisy Repeating Rifle, must have gotten it when he was eight or nine years old, like most of us kids. The BBs keep bouncing around, like someone was throwing little pebbles down from the sky, most of them harmless, but an occasional one getting enough velocity that they'd stick in something. Meanwhile, folks started getting tired of holding the parade up, and began drifting away, with the deputy directing traffic down to the park.

When Billy realized that the parade was breaking up, he stood up and started calling for Reese, "the Nazi butcher," to come back. Finally, he was so mad, he started threatening everyone in sight, saying he was going home for a real gun, his dad's .22, if they didn't listen, and warning them not to eat Bluebell. His parents, everyone noticed, had kept out of sight, because on a day when their other two sons had done such a fine job, Billy had to go and embarrass everyone, so they were trying to ignore him like a whiney child, I guess. By the time the sheriff and deputy had put their horses away and gotten back, a group of local men had gathered a block away to discuss what to do with Billy. Everyone else was down at the river having a drink and savoring the smell of the nearly done, crisping pork they would soon be eating.

Some of the younger men wanted Mr. Bond and his sons to climb up there and take Billy down forcibly, and kept muttering about what a disgrace it was to have a kid making such a big fuss in front of the whole town. Mr. Bond looked pretty uncomfortable, but kept his silence. I don't think he trusted Billy not to shoot him with the BB gun as he came over the top. Besides, he was sick of Billy's moping around about the damn hog anyway. "I'll leave it up to the sheriff," was all he'd say. Then the men turned to the sheriff and asked what he intended to do.

The sheriff looked around him, hooked his thumbs in his belt and announced, "Nothing. I'm going to get a beer and some food now, and if Billy Bond wants to sit on that roof all the rest of his life, he can." Then as he moved through the group, he added, "But I bet he'll be down by the time snow falls." And true to his word, he went to the park, got himself a beer and started flirting with the younger women, like he always did. Some of the men tried to get up energy to go get Billy after that, but the heart was gone out of it, and the town just went on and celebrated the homecoming, drinking beer and eating roast pig.

I liked Billy, but I tried not to think about him up there alone on the bank roof, probably sobbing his heart out while the rest of the folks were down there eating his

Bluebell. "Things have to go on in life," that's what people told each other that night. "You can't take on so about a mere animal; you have to know that they're here for people to eat. This is a good experience for him," they told each other, and his dad promised he'd get a good whipping once he got off that roof. So everyone felt pretty good, and I didn't even mind so much being with my sister Baby on my first date. She got so wrapped up in the food, like I knew she would, and Kenton was careful to get someone to keep supplying her with big full plates while he and I snuck off with some of the other kids our age to the dance. All in all, it was a fine homecoming, and even Reese got to laughing about the BB in his arm by the end of the evening.

No one gave Billy Bond a thought as we drifted back home around eleven that night. The big bonfire that'd been built down on the riverbank was starting to die down, but its aroma filled the cold fall air with a wonderful burning wood smell. And I guess we just assumed he'd gotten down and walked back to the farm—that is, if we thought about him at all.

The next day, when Billy hadn't shown up by one o'clock, after church services were out, and no one had heard a word from the roof, the sheriff and his deputy did go up there to see if they could find him. He was there alright, sitting in the corner, hugging himself like he was still cold from the hard frost we'd had overnight, but when the men tried to talk him into standing up and coming home, he'd looked up at them with a face as white as milk—that's what they'd said, he was just gone. There wasn't anything left in him, so they'd carried and dragged him down the ladder to the street below and carted him off home. But it didn't do any good. A few days later, as we were going to school one morning, there goes the deputy driving by the high school with Mr. Bond beside him in front, and Billy Bond sitting in the back still hugging himself, looking out the window with a face like an empty bowl. And when I waved, he looked at me like I was the man in the moon.

Aronson's Orchard

And in the fall, it is being haunted by the dried vines that have left their darker mark along the wooden fence behind the house on the farm I remember as my first home. I think we were happy there. Now I don't know for sure. I'm haunted by the orange globes that dot the dying-out garden to the left of the biggest barn, the pumpkins that lie there in wait for us a week before Halloween when we'll be out to pull them in, carve them up and give the extras to the neighbors. We don't have to hide them the way we do the watermelon patch, which kids spend half their summer nights trying to discover, driving slowly along the little back roads hoping to spot a clearing, a scarecrow, the aluminum pie plates strung on a rope along the edge back near the woods. Sometimes they'll spend a week watching for the farmer to make his move toward the beloved watermelon patch. The next morning, the melons are gone—only the rinds of those eaten on the spot litter the area. But by October the kids have lost interest in the hunt. They're back at school, back at football, and back at each other.

In the fall here in Divinity, it is being haunted by the sight of those dark red, almost mahogany apples at

Aronson's Orchard. Aronson's great-great-grandfather had brought the first seedlings over from the Old Country, wrapped in burlap and secreted among his belongings. Every day he'd unwrap them, slip them out for sun, cupping each in his hand like a kitten, so that by the time he'd landed, he was ready to start his apple orchard. He'd always told the other farmers that came out with him, "First you plant the trees. A tiny house for you to live in, then the trees. A man must leave his mark on the land so the future will know him." But the neighbors always figured they could get their apples from Aronson. Eventually he planted enough trees to keep the growing community, and opened his orchard officially. Although it had always been his intention to start dairy farming, not apple farming, he just never got around to doing more than slowly building one big barn and acquiring a single cow. Over the years his descendants carried on the same routine: trading apples and other fruit for the produce and meat they needed, then selling the surplus to the suppliers of large stores in the cities.

Curiously, they always kept just one cow, as if the old man, the first Aronson, had set a precedent they couldn't break. After a while the barn was put to use for storage and processing, and more recently, Aronson's cleaned it up inside for the customers he has coming from all over to buy apples and see his little "apple museum." During the apple season, from late August to January, older women come in to bake their best apple pies. Usually these are women whose husbands are retired or dead, and they can use the extra work and cash. At first it was just a couple, like Tom Tooley's mom, but after a while it became such a popular thing, those pies—and you can buy them fresh, baked, or frozen, they're all good—that people would stop and buy one at the drop of a hat all fall, just for dinner. Then last year he added homemade cinnamon ice cream, and that's real good, too, on hot pie. This year he's making donuts and trying out apple muffins.

Each year, Aronson feels like he has to improve something. "It's part of the old-world tradition," he tells folks. "You have to keep working on it, making it a little better year after year."

Aronson once came to our high school for career lectures and explained how the apple trees are only productive for a certain amount of time, then you have to have another batch of trees coming up alongside so when you dig out the old tree, the new tree is ready to go. Aronson swears by the strain his great-great-grandfather brought over. Still uses it. He's worried that all the dinking around they do to dwarf trees, to make them higher yield and blight, insect and weather resistant is ruining the flavor of the apple. Aronson keeps trying to do it the old way, but he's having trouble getting people to help him, he says; young people don't want to work that hard. But he's not down on us like other folks around here. He still feels awful, you know, after what happened to his son Reinhardt.

Everyone has a theory in Divinity. They always have and always will. Theories and opinions and dreams. With a few historical facts thrown in. And lots of memories. Reinhardt Aronson is one of those people who produced more than his share of all of these. Twyla makes a face and orders another drink whenever his name comes up, and it never does unless we're in a bar. That's one thing about Reinhardt: you don't mention him at the dining room table or in the presence of small children. Twyla's encounter with him wasn't as bad as it could have been— that's what everyone says. She says she could have lived without any of it, wished she had, too. Another thing about Reinhardt is that no one mentions his name to old man Aronson, and if his wife had lived, to her either. Although the old man makes a trip to Anamosa to see

Reinhardt once a year, it just doesn't do much good. I don't know who he'll leave that orchard to—Reinhardt won't come back here afterwards, that's for sure.

Some of the opinions around here hold that Aronson worked Reinhardt too much, too early—and that's unusual, coming from a farming community where as soon as you're old enough to walk, you start getting your chores. People can understand farm work, that's one thing, but tree work, that's another. Picking the apples, backbreaking work, is something you should hire out to migrants, but Aronson would never do that, didn't believe the apples would be treated right.

Other people say that it was in the genes—that's the genealogists, of course, Baby and her crowd. Too much inbreeding. Reinhardt was bound to come along sooner or later. They're worried. Maybe they'll get a Reinhardt of their own one of these days. Maybe some of them already have. Like my brother EuGene maybe. Some of them luckily got killed in Vietnam, where the families sent them to grow up or die. Of course, no one would ever say that out loud. But there seems to be a good chance that growing up can kill you the way it's done around here.

Whatever the cause, old man Aronson lets the kids who work for him get away with murder. Maybe that's only since Reinhardt, or maybe he was always too nice to his son. Should have cracked him, instead of trying to be understanding all the time. The problem was that no one seemed to let Reinhardt know that he wasn't doing everything just right. Even the teachers at school tended to let Reinhardt get away with things. There was something that made him get a talking-to, while someone like Clinton got the ruler across his butt. I think Clinton knew pretty much that Reinhardt was going to get away with everything in life, because he didn't spend much time with him after a while, although they were cousins.

Reinhardt Aronson looked like a god, or better yet, like a prince. That's what a teacher told him once—like a Bavarian prince. It stuck, and we called him Prince, like he was someone's pet horse. He took to believing it after a while, too, pushing what he'd always done anyway a little more. Taking his turn first, taking advantage, but always with that clear, bold way that reminded you of someone in the movies, playing royalty, always shoving in front of everyone else and not even looking around to see if everyone fell back the way they should. And we did. It seemed natural to give way before Prince Reinhardt with his golden hair and hard, handsome face. There were moments that reinforced it too: like the times Reinhardt had to beat someone up and would do it in a particularly vicious fashion, continuing to punch and kick long after the other boy had clearly finished. It left a little pinched place in your memory to watch that, and after a couple of times, nobody bothered him.

Although there were lots of rumors about him by the time we were in junior high, the story about Reinhardt and the cat was the first thing that made us really wonder about him. Clinton said Reinhardt had showed the boys how to stick their finger up a cat in heat to relieve it. It was Jimmy got caught doing it and slapped around pretty good by his father. But you know, the cats would take to following a boy who tried it. They'd know whoever had done that to them, they'd want more. Maybe that's what gave Reinhardt encouragement, because the next thing he tried was chickens. It just went on from there. In high school he started in with anything he could put himself inside, according to Clinton. While his dad was out working in the orchard, he'd be in the little stall with the cow, showing the other boys how to do it. It was enough to make me sick, let me tell you. They say some of those boys giggled and made jokes with the Prince.

After a while, when animals weren't enough, he started on girls.

Most of us girls had gotten wind of what Reinhardt did, and wouldn't go near him. Handsome and having all the spending money he wanted, he'd still have to recruit girls from other towns or go with the wild ones. Either way, it'd always end up the same. He was a little too rough, a little too demanding, and they'd drop him after a date or two and go around wearing this little hurt expression, feeling sorry about something—maybe themselves. Once during a dance in our junior year there was a big fuss in the parking lot outside the high school because Reinhardt had dragged Babette Ponder into the back of his father's big Oldsmobile ninety-eight and torn off half her clothes. She'd had a few drinks and her guard was down. Probably thought it'd be a good trick to pull on her boyfriend she was having a fight with or something. But Reinhardt wasn't satisfied with making out and tore her blouse trying to get at her, and if she hadn't developed a healthy set of lungs, he probably would have torn off the rest of her clothes.

All hell broke loose, and Reinhardt finally just shoved Babette out of the car to the waiting arms of her boyfriend and a gathering crowd, then jumped in the front seat, started the car and rammed it through the lot before anyone figured out that they should pound him into the pavement. I remember the way everyone stood there, mouths dropping, frozen in the receding red of the taillights, with Babette still crouching where he'd thrown her, the knees of her nylons torn out, the skin bloody raw from being scraped on the concrete, and her red silk blouse hanging by a couple of threads from its collar, with one arm poking out naked and tender. You could almost see the imprint of his fingers on the flesh, the way they would be when she showed everyone in the bathroom on Monday morning at school. And we all wore that same dumb look you saw on the villagers' faces in a Dracula movie.

I don't know why we never said anything to our parents. We just didn't. Maybe we were ashamed, like being caught in a situation with Reinhardt was our own fault. There were always wild girls to go out with him though, to match him—or to try to match him—at whatever he wanted to do. People at school said that he'd already knocked up a girl in Osceola, but that was just rumor. It was always someone's cousin who heard it, or it happened to, but never really a related person. And for some reason, there were always girls who took chances with Reinhardt, as if it were some kind of test they wanted very badly to pass—going out with Reinhardt and coming back unscathed, hot and bold with their bragging that they'd put him in his place, he hadn't got to base one with them. Everyone wants to walk into the mouth of the lion and back out. Some of them even made it. I know that our boyfriends used to tease and threaten us with Reinhardt, and sometimes we'd both pretend and let ourselves go. It was fun once in a while to feel that way, like all the controls were gone.

When we graduated from high school, Reinhardt went away for a while, first to college, but we heard that he left there, then to Vietnam, but he didn't stay there long either. We couldn't imagine him taking orders. Anyway, he was one of the first back, and by then his father couldn't do anything about him. Reinhardt just took over the family car until the old man bought him his own, and spent the nights and days when he wasn't sleeping out on the roads looking for women, drinking and fighting. It's not like there was any direct proof for a long time. I mean, no one charged him with any of it. He was careful, too. He didn't touch children. I think women had become his meat finally.

At first he operated well outside of here, and since most of them were too embarrassed to report it even, he was free to do it again. Before long, though, the stories about people's cousins, then sisters and wives were piling up so high that we had to start believing them. About that time he was getting lazy, staying closer to home. I think, in fact, that Twyla was about the first he tried right here in town. She was lucky. When he popped up out of the back seat on the outskirts of town late one fall afternoon, holding a knife to her neck and telling her he'd "kill her if she didn't stop the car and fuck him," she told him to go ahead—she'd had a lousy day anyway. This surprised him so much that he jumped out when she slowed down for a stop sign at Highway 11 and the entrance to our road.

Twyla sat there for a few minutes laughing her guts out, then panicked and drove to my place. By the time she stepped out of the car, she was shaking all over and bawling her head off. Jake was out of town and Tom was out and about, so we just sat there at my little kitchen table, the door locked and a chair shoved under the knob to make us feel more secure, in case he'd followed her.

At first we were going to tell the sheriff, call him right up, but then the more we talked about it, the more we realized that he'd probably think she was lying, because everyone thought Twyla and I were the biggest runarounds in town. Reinhardt would just deny it, of course, then wait to catch her alone again. After we'd come to that, we started drinking, and by ten o'clock we were so drunk we could almost laugh about it. That's what we did that night: made jokes and passed out at midnight.

They found Carla's body about six A.M., when Bevington went to milk his cows. She was tied to one of the stanchions, carved up good, and dead. They found the knife outside the barn in some dried weeds that had been trampled down, and the tire tracks up the back way through his pasture. The rest was simple. Reinhardt was sleeping it off at home, and the old man didn't put up so much as a single word. I think he'd known all along something was going to happen. Mrs. Aronson collapsed silently and died the next day. According to Mel Weller, the deputy, the Prince didn't even want to go to the funeral. I don't think he bothered much with family feeling.

When Twyla had to go in and testify about the knife, I went with her. It was something. The description of the body was enough to make you sick. The sheriff said she looked like a piece of fresh veal after the job Reinhardt had done. Reinhardt still looked like a prince at the trial, we were just the dumb villagers who would be tended to later. Old man Aronson looked a lot older, his face engraved with worry that never went away after that. The last thing Reinhardt sneered to him was, "Go fuck yourself."

Tom made a big deal of swaggering around the bars after that, claiming that he was going to get Reinhardt if he wasn't sent up for good. Finally he quieted down when Twyla reminded him that he'd been out screwing around when he should have been home to protect her that night. Reinhardt got sixty years in Anamosa for killing Carla Ross, and he's up for parole in twenty, but I doubt he'll get it. When the trial came up, the sheriff started getting a lot of phone calls from all over the place, telling him things Reinhardt had done. Most of them were anonymous, but they were enough to make him have a talk in private with the judge about the Prince, and I guess the judge had a talk with the prison, so he's not getting out till he's seventy at least. Deputy Weller made sure everyone knew that, and you know, it was comforting, for a change, to hear his gossip.

It took old man Aronson a few years to get over losing his wife and son, to get over feeling like we all thought *he'd* done it, not Reinhardt. I think what convinced him, finally, was that people showed up the next fall for the apples, just like always. But the following year, you could see his whole body lift up and his face get a little brighter when he realized that we weren't just coming back there for the curiosity, but that we really wanted the apples we had come to depend on him growing. The best, the sweetest, the deepest-blood-red apples you can find. At Aronson's Orchard, down Old Quarry Road, right off Highway 11. And every year there's something added, like another apology to us all. Apple dumplings, apple cider, apple donuts, apple dolls, and always and always, apples. The hardest and juiciest of which he saves back each fall for the truckload he'll bring up to Anamosa at Christmastime for Prince Reinhardt, who never sees him.

At Last

And then the day came when there was no more. First the grasses yellowed in places, stopped growing. There was no need to cut the lawns after that, until all of them lay flat and brown as in February. But it was June now. We watched the garden flowers begin to wilt—the blooms came slow and dusty, small fists of effort, then the buds merely burned on their drying stems. The tomato and bean plants dried from the bottom up: each week another layer of leaves dangled limp and yellow from the vine. The hollyhocks bursting tall like long fingers into the sky, six or seven feet, frozen in the heat. Later they waved in the wind, dead sticks, nearly empty seedpods rattling on the stalks. We expected rain each week, as we always did in this place, thought it would come, piling dark on the eastern sky or blowing up from the gulf—but each day passed and then another.

The five-lined skink laid more and more often where we could see him out in the shade of the woodpile. There were no cups of moisture in the vines about the stone foundation of the house. More and more the trees and bushes sought their own economy—dropping leaves to protect themselves from the vast drying air.

Even the birds, previously only heard with a musical chirruping in the woods, began to move closer to us: a hummingbird searching for the flowers of our bushes, which would not come now, a downy woodpecker, the wrens hopping along the porch, all looking for the least drop of moisture. Not even a night dew now.

Every day the sky, a blue. Nothing more. Nothing less. Then we began to find the turtles: the large ones, two or three times bigger than a hand with spread fingers. In the drying woods we could stumble over their shells, humped like rocks among the dead leaves, discover their decaying bodies inside. We found five of them that way before we realized what was happening—an omen we felt; though not by nature superstitious, we knew this to be a sign. The turtles, even the terrestrial ones, living on the moisture from the foliage and insect bodies, lost, lost in some amazement—the surprise of a forest turning desert. Even the water holes long sucked dry by the thirsty air.

It was then, too, that we noticed the insects, their unusual voraciousness, their hunger for sweat and blood, some liquid, of our animals, of ourselves. At night they netted our bodies with their constant motion, the continual seeking for pores like tiny pools where their drinking could take place. But often they lacked the strength. Bobbing along the ceiling, they would suddenly drop— by morning the beds were dotted with their black and gray forms. We noticed, too, that the spiders, especially the larger ones, began to spin webs in strange and erratic patterns. A certain disorientation seemed to occur. And the webs themselves, filling with the weaker moths and flies, often went unattended. Later when we searched the nest, we would find the spider, brittle legs bent stiffly or outspread in an awkward position, its body sunken and papery.

We would find even the larger moths each morning, the pale luna and the polyphemus, the sphinx—all the magical ones—dead on the porches and windowsills. Drawn by our lights through the dark, they spent their last energy beating large, delicate wings slowly against the screens.

There were no butterflies to speak of, and after a while, even the tree frogs were silent in the long night heat. We did not examine the trees then. Although it was the time for seven-year locusts to come mottling out of the ground, we no longer heard their harsh whistle. The birds, too, grew more sluggish. It was possible, finally, to walk within a few inches of a cardinal perched on the wilted bushes along the drive. Speckled thrashers continued to hunt for grapes in the arbor, unable to understand, it seemed, that those hard, nutty berries clustered in the drying vines were the only crop now.

It was not that we became friends then—the animals and the humans—but that we were no longer independent of each other.

After we had begun to urinate in the woods (the toilets no longer usable, only a trickle of water plumbed through the pipes from the emptying well), we realized that our body excrement could nurture some of the smaller insects and plants—those surviving the acidic burns. At this point, it had been so long after all, we were aware that while we had always taken the animal noises and their presence, as well, for granted, still the absence of that variety of whistles and hutterings left us with a kind of blankness, a silence full of longing and fear. At times, we would have willingly opened a vein to feed these creatures. Surrounded by their death and by the relentless heat, we entered a new stage of mourning. Somehow it mattered less that we were alive, so haunted were we by the silence. We knew that when the wind stopped—as we also knew it must, even the blistering one that threw waves of glowing hot air over our bodies until we almost drowned in it—we knew that when the trees stopped rustling and rattling, and the houses stopped creaking as of under great strain, then that would be the last of it. To have the only sound a human one of body against bush, of self clapping onto self, the only sound an extension of ourselves, would be our death. Perfect stillness. The dream of our life, would kill us.

The Geographers

She could not remember more than the mare standing in the sun glazing her body with sweat and the flies biting her hard, each one drawing blood, and the man holding her head gently and sorrowfully stroking her nose, trying to shield her eyes from the insects. The vet held a large vial of clear liquid up into the sunlight, inserted a needle and pulled the plunger back. He turned toward the mare, tapped her twice on the neck and pushed the needle into the vein. The liquid drained from the tube into her neck. When he pulled the needle out, a drop of blood oozed to the skin, glistened bright red against her brown coat. The vet stepped back, patted her side and walked away. He turned once and said to the man, she'll go down in a minute or so. Then he left, backing the car slowly down the steep and rocky pasture road, across the tiny stream and back up through the gate and away.

The child sat on the hill opposite the mare, staring intently. She was not going to miss anything. The woman and the man waited. In a moment the horse's eyes began to flutter, she panicked, fighting the drug, breathing heavily through her nostrils, trying to snort away the bad smell in her body. The woman watched as the mare's knees buckled all at once and she went down first in front and then in back. She sat awkwardly for a moment, her weight resting on her knees and back legs, her eyes half shut. With a deep groan, she rolled over and settled on her side, her legs twitched, her eyelids drifted shut, her breath came out in quiet shallow gulps and then not at all.

The man was still standing with the end of the lead rope in his hands, looking at the horse. The flies swiftly covered her face. The child looked away and then down at the stones beside her. The man dropped the rope at the nose of the horse, turned and began walking down the pasture road. Stopped when he saw the rusty red truck pulling in front of the gate. Ran up to open the pasture gate and waved the driver on. The truck swayed over the rocky path and drove just beyond where the horse lay on the hillside.

A man got out, walked to the back of the truck, switched on the electric pulley, dragged the cable down to the horse. He bent over, undid the halter and rope, threw them to one side and attached the cable in a loop around her neck. The flies, undisturbed, settled on her face and neck again as he walked back to the truck and moved the lever into a forward position. The auxiliary engine made a thin whirring sound as it pulled in the slack on the cable. The horse began to move as the cable was drawn into its housing. The people watched as the stiffening body was dragged up into the truck. Finally it rested terribly, with its head drawn up and its neck stretched out. The weight of its body on the bed of the truck. The driver turned, got into the truck and began to back down the road. The man stared at the spot where the mare had lain. The child watched the truck. The woman moved away from the window in the kitchen and sat down at the table.

A Farm Story

She was walking toward the henhouse—a small white structure with four wire windows on each side open now for summer ventilation. The afternoon was so hot she could hardly breathe the damp air. The chickens, giving up on the day, nested in the cool straw boxes or in the powdery dirt under the plum thicket—a density she never dared enter, the spiked twigs tearing her hair, scratching her face, hardly worth the two or three eggs she could recover. Sparrows were the real nuisance of the farm. Her husband hired a boy to smash the eggs each spring, but he never got all of them. There were always the same number of ugly brown birds stealing grain or fighting with the barn swallows that lived in the toolshed. Her husband and she liked the swallows at dusk. When the animals were quiet at last, they watched the dark arrow shapes dipping over the barnyard and into the sheds—a nightly dance to close the day.

She went up one step, stooped for the low doorway and walked into the ammonia smell of bird crap and disinfectant, making her pull in for a moment. Every piece of wood was stained with droppings, and in some places under favorite roosting racks, it piled in white pyramids to be scraped out twice a year. Her eyes grew used to the dim light as she turned toward the rows of nests. Several hens sat dozing or watching her with black round eyes. She hated this part. She hated putting her hand under their bodies to gather the eggs they were warming. She hated the fear she felt. The quick jab of the beak into her hand or arm—the anger, the fear—it was her ordeal every day to come down here. Once she had worn a pair of her husband's work gloves, but they were too stiff and heavy for her. She had to use her own hands, unprotected. It was also the warmth: she hated the blood feeling between the soft feathers and the hard eggs.

Sliding her fingers beneath the first hen, she got two eggs safely out and into the basket. There were three eggs in the next empty box. That was best. Eggs without chicken, she laughed to herself at the old joke. OK. So far so good. The next hen was awake and alert. It made a small jerk toward her hand but settled down when she said "no." She could never quite be sure how smart the birds were—whether she should bother at all trying to speak to them as she did the other animals. The dogs and cats, of course. The horse listened, she knew, for a carrot or apple—an exchange of information. Steers were stupid—no getting around that. She avoided them in the pastures. Even felt superior to their indifference. She had never petted one. She hated the animals raised for food. Their absolute stupidity. The abuse they suffered. At times, though, she caught herself talking to the hens as she threw the afternoon scraps out—laughing as they fought over the vegetable peels. She must be careful never to throw out eggshells, her husband said, it makes hens crave eggs. They begin to eat their own, picking small holes in the shells and drinking the contents. Then they had to be killed. Nothing worse than an eggeater.

She gathered ten more eggs successfully. She glanced into the next box; an egg shone out of the darkness. Good. No chicken to fight with. She stuck her hand in.

Something. Cool and smooth and hard. No. A low buzz. Bees. No. Pull the hand out. Egg slowly dissolves into darkness. Outline now. The bullet head. A fat body coiled around and around, she knew. The eye like a chicken's— shiny and hard. A step back. Guts twist now. Trembling. Hand useless. Dirty. God. Goddamn it. Goddamn it. Goddamn it. Something—a stone, no, the pitchfork, no her husband's gun. No, be reasonable, the pitchfork standing just inside the door. She moved without a sound— not even the rustle of straw on the floor. Set the egg basket down. Pitchfork in hand now. Over to box. Which one. There. There it is, see the eye. Both hands grip the wooden handle's lightness. Up into the box, into straw snap of body, push harder snap of fork, writhing snake, uncoiled spring broken, curved pieces scattered in the straw. Blood eye. Look, I see myself buried in the snake, its blackness my blood coating straw, staining the egg red and yellow, now broken coils, broken shells, brittle straw. Look at it—stab it again—look at it—there's nothing but darkness sucking the prongs of the fork. There's the chicken: you gutted its black stupid eye. You burst its soft body, you let in the straw hard and dead and yellow, there is nothing, nothing here. I have hidden in the bull snake folded on the rafters above the door in the toolshed.

She turned again to the door. Placed the pitchfork carefully against the wall, prongs down for safety. And walked down into the barnyard again and toward the house. As her form cleared the darkness from the doorway, a snake edged toward the basket of eggs still sitting in the light.

Emma May Sievert

In March the calves start coming. You can hear them bawling in the clear, late-night air, the sound magnified and projected by the barn's interior, the mother an anxious prisoner in the stanchion up the aisle, stamping and backing against the metal noose like a car stuck in mud. The snow has started to melt with the arrival of warmer days, and though we know the storms aren't over for good, we welcome the brown patches that rise up like new islands in the white ocean that surrounds us. It's a small thing, I know, but somehow it becomes the signal for those who held out all the dark days through the desolation of January and February, when the sky froze like a new enamel pan capping anything that moved on the ground below it. We know this because every year about this time, someone just can't wait any longer. May is hard for folks, too, but it's March that really signals the beginning of the new year.

Emma May Sievert probably just went down for preserves like always, you know, to the part of the basement beneath the stairs, dug in against the little hill the house sat on. Her husband's family had been in that house for a good eighty, one hundred years. At first they'd burned wood, then coal, finally oil. So maybe the root cellar was once the coal bin. It was dark enough. How do I know? I do, I can tell you. We know everything about each other here, everything about our neighbors' houses, the glimpses we catch the times we're inside, or things we hear someone talk about it. Nothing passes away here, everything is saved, like the town is an enormous attic where everybody contributes what's to be kept for the future, for another person to use, another generation. Or just in case, we don't throw a thing away. So yes, I did know about the root cellar that was dark enough. And I can tell you that Emma wasn't fond of going down there, mostly got the kids to go once they passed the danger of falling off the stairs. Siggert was always going to put the handrail back up—you know he meant to—but he had so much to do. That's a fact. That farm took all his time plus more. A man couldn't do everything alone, no hired help but at harvest, and then the kind of men Emma May fed on big improvised tables from planks kept in the dusty rafters of the barn set on sawhorses out in the backyard. Not the kind of men she'd even dream of inviting into the dining room, to eat off the special hand-crocheted tablecloth spread over the old Irish linen she'd saved from her mother, who'd saved it from *her* mother. The lace covered the tiny threads starting to poke out in little holes.

Siggert was the talker in that family. Emma May, she served the meals, did the house chores, took care of the chickens, the vegetable garden, the flowers, fed the new calves, but it was Siggert did the talking. Always acting like they were in a fancy restaurant. Even in town visiting or shopping, he'd tell what she wanted: "Emma May would like a spool of that thread there, ma'am." Or "Emma May will have another cup of coffee and a tiny slice of that pineapple upside-down, please." She wasn't a mute, of course, and when she got off by herself with some of the other ladies, well, she had some of her say, not a lot, mind you, but some. So we didn't figure Siggert was pressing the lid down on her or anything. Emma May liked things that way. "Siggert Politeness," I guess you'd call it. Like a lady didn't have to speak in public unless she wanted to. Now that I think on it, it was probably Siggert told us about the root cellar and Emma not liking to go down there. And the kids, in the manner of courtesy their papa used, did it for her. Yes, that's right, the kids acted the same way, polite to their mama, as if she was special and you needed to be real quiet and sweet with her, like new-born chickens or ducks you didn't want to frighten.

I don't know why Siggert had so many early calves that year. Probably just an accident, the three coming right away. His herd was big enough so he could spread out the freshening through to June, and have plenty to do. But the three calves—you can imagine the moaning they set up those first few days. The mama cows calling so it sounded like human sobbing as the noise drifted up across the fields, lifting itself like it was being carried by flocks of birds that'd settle right onto the roof of your house, so that you'd hear that ungodly sound everywhere, the cows and their babies that'd been taken right away from them, put on the bucket so the mamas could be milked again. And you could just see the babies, tugging so hard at the pieces of baling twine that held them around the necks, tied to the stanchions in the dark barn while the mamas milled around outside during the day, rolling their eyes, and sticking their wide noses up in the air to let out the most sad, the most tearful sound a human being could ever expect to hear, their heavy bags swinging painfully against their legs, calling for the little fellows to come out and nurse, like they were supposed to. Inside, the babies squealing and tugging, panting, finally broken out in a sweat because they're so afraid and the rope is burning through their new hair. Like they know. You think they know, especially the bull calves, what it means when the farmer loads them into his stock trailer, half carrying them up the little ramp, half kicking and lifting them, the farmer's curses mingling with the calves bawling and bellering like a bunch of pigs at feeding time.

Emma May never said anything about it, but you could imagine the pain it must have caused a quiet woman like herself, a woman whose own children played in hushed tones so she wouldn't be disturbed, whose own chickens seemed to cluck softer and kinder, from some inborn knowledge that Emma did prefer it that way, though she'd never say. Anyway, all the kids were in school during the days. She'd be up at four thirty to start chores, fix the food, get them ready for the bus that'd pick them up down at the end of the driveway. The kids did the calves in the morning, and she did them other times during the day. But you know she must have been up all the nights before with that racket coming from the barn, like the moon had blown into pieces and dropped a huge sliver of its glassy light through the roof into her bedroom. She must have been wrestling with it all night, trying to dislodge that noise that stabbed so and pinned her to that bed, next to the sleeping Siggert. A good man. He never woke up.

I don't think it was more than a mistake that Siggert took the calves without telling her. She might not have heard him say he was taking them that day. Life together is like that, isn't it. After a while, you think you're talking out loud to each other, and all you're doing is carrying on the conversation in your head, you've got the sound of each other's voice set so in there. And you would think that the temperature that day in March—right up to sixty—that that would have kept her upstairs, or outside cleaning the hen house, or walking the path to the Mercy River that ran through the back pasture to see if it was jammed from all the melting. You'd think that, wouldn't you?

She must have meant to be baking—something special for the kids that day when they got home, little cakes squatting in pools of preserved plums. Emma made the best plum preserves around. When there was an occasion, you always hoped she'd bring them to your house. We never told her that, wouldn't want to intrude on her manners, but we sure looked forward to the taste of those plums. Half jam, half fruit. If you were really lucky, you'd pull out a long violet strand on the end of your spoon and smear it around your toast or biscuit. I swear, it was better than a candy bar.

Anyway, I don't think she'd gotten used to the calves bawling, so she would have missed them right away. Or maybe, as I sometimes see it, she stood with her face pressed against the cool wood of the door frame, turned so she looked out the glass inset at the top of the door. She'd be able to watch the loading without Siggert seeing her—like unruly children being shoved in a car by their tired parents. Which of us hasn't seen that, hasn't thought of it that way? The stubborn legs locked against compliance, the flail of arms, the heads jerked up so the faces could be slapped, the small backs frail against the dark hollow of the back door opening. She would have seen and heard it before. But it was March and three bull calves. The hard luck of it. The first three and not a heifer among them. The sudden silence. What she might have gone to the root cellar for, the jar of plum preserves in her right hand, the silence in her other.

Siggert explaining that the price of veal might drop, the way they'd gotten used to hearing reports coming over the radio, rising and falling about their house like a tide whose mysterious rhythm was as distant as the moon.

In May you see the trucks on the highway going back and forth, filled with livestock bought and sold. All over the countryside life gets noisier with tractors putt-putting into the night, the hatchings, whelpings, birthings rising up with the new damp smell released from the soil that is turned and turned again. Until frost the insects and the birds and the frogs combine so there is never a truly quiet moment, day or night. It's what you have to get used to again, each year, that feeling that something is buzzing in your ear until the cold clamps down on you like a freezer lid being shut.

I don't know. It happened sometime that morning in the dark center of the root cellar under the basement stairs, the walls lined with unfinished plank shelves, stained by dark and damp, on which rested last summer's work, jar after jar she would remember the labor of. The small cuts and scaldings. The insect bites and the bruises. The exhaustion with her body soaked in sweat and sweet steamed fruit. The nausea persistent in the kitchen those last weeks of harvesting corn and beets and tomatoes and grapes and squash and beans and plums, always the plums. Until the cooking plums seemed to separate into strands of red, raw meat that she almost mistook for chickens she must gut and prepare for dinner, for men would be in soon from the fields and kids were nowhere to be found. The plums swimming like small bloody fish in the stew pan on the stove, as if there was no way to catch and bottle them, as if she would have to kill each one of them first before they could be of use.

You know how people are, they settle on an idea and put it on like it's the last suit of clothes they own. Siggert, he somehow decided it was her heart. Maybe the doctor told him that. Lots of people die of a sudden without getting murdered, at least around here it's that way. Her heart, he'd say solemnly, nodding his head up and down like a perpetual drinking rooster on the kitchen counter—you know, you probably brought one home from the same county-fair booth I did. It made sense, everyone working to keep quiet around her. Then, of course, Ranberg, the fertilizer man from Pottersville who had been going to deliver that afternoon, just after the kids came home from school and went down to the basement freezer for ice cream. He found the cellar door open, and her sitting in there, propped up like a lady at a tea party. He said there was a gun. Now he didn't say whether she used it or not. Just that there was one. Told his wife that, and she told her hairdresser, who called over and told Twyla, who told me. A gun. Have to be a pistol, that's what I thought at first. Emma May was too much of a lady for a shotgun or rifle. Of course there'd be one handy— on a farm you never knew when you'd have to finish something. She might have carried it down to scare off the field rats that lurked in the cellar. Then as I thought about it more, I realized that if she was sitting on that cold dirt floor to begin with, she might not object to something as awkward as a shotgun. It might be just the ticket, but I don't think so. Probably it was just her heart, after all.

I once heard about a woman who killed her whole family with the stewed tomatoes. Waited until she'd had quite enough, fixed them a big bowlful one cold winter night, and they were gone by morning. Botulism. She'd marked the jars carefully so they'd be there when she needed them. Years before. Only Emma'd never want to hurt anyone. She'd probably only meant to get a little peace and quiet down there. I think I can understand that, closing her eyes with the treasured plums in one hand resting in her lap, the rest of the fruit gradually spilling out into the cup of dress, maybe just as she drifted off, the plums came alive again and she forgave them. The other hand pressing the packed dirt floor to steady the rocking house until she was asleep.

Heat Wave

The house was losing numbers again and box elder bugs clung to the hot wire of the screen like they were going down for the third time. Every time it got hot enough, the big wooden numbers the former owners had bought and stuck on with some thick black adhesive to make the place more contemporary, slid off the stucco an inch at a time until there were long black skids down the front of the house. Sunny glanced at her white legs, dappled with sweat pimples and creases from the sheets of her afternoon nap. They looked like the whole Midwest to her—stricken by drought, reduced to bumps and stubbles of fields. She shivered with the heat and wondered if her husband, Mr. Smith, (recently, Sunny had taken to calling him Mr. Smith) would rather she dieted or went along and ate it out with him.

Whenever the temperature got stuck like a gas pedal to the floor, winter or summer, Sunny's husband ate to the accompaniment of the TV weather channel, like a prophet waiting out the end of the world. Surrounded by his books on chaos and time, he watched the maps roll by, filled with the warning red of 100 plus, day after day, placidly, almost with contentment.

"River's down another foot," he announced each night before they went to bed. He hadn't touched her since the drought started. She hadn't wanted him to either. She couldn't imagine how she ever had sex in the summer before, with two bodies sliding in sweat. While Sunny grew more restless in the heat, sleeping in short bursts that seemed more like gunfire, Mr. Smith slept separate, like a roommate.

Three days before the river bottom appeared, she saw the blackbirds in the backyard searching numbly through the yellow grass for water or food, then squatting with their beaks parted, their small, dark slivers of tongue visible as they panted in the 105-degree afternoon. When Sunny broke the ban on watering to sprinkle them, they flew away.

"I can't believe you're watering blackbirds," Mr. Smith said and took her box of Better Cheddars from the shelf. They had divided the crackers: he got stone grounds and anything pale and sweet. But when he ran out and the weather turned bad, he took her Better Cheddars.

"River dropped four feet today," he said into the dark jar of their bedroom that night and put a pillow between them so they wouldn't get hot from touching. "We'll see bottom in a few days."

Sunny knew they should have gotten married in a wedding chapel in Las Vegas. That was one of the observations she made when it got hot. Then she'd be able to go to a hotel when he slept downstairs where it was cooler. Instead, they'd done the church bit, marching down the aisle like they'd earned it, taken it home with the paycheck and the job benefit package. Now they lived like husband and wife. It was shocking. He let her clean the toilet, the tub. He took out the garbage. The only thing they did together was the garden, and she did the watering. They'd just eaten their first watermelon together. Like their marriage, it was only half ripe. After the ritual cutting, he took the reddest part of the dark green melon shaped like a half-inflated volleyball, and left her the yellow and pink side. "Save the seeds," he ordered.

Today, Sunny decided, was the day for the goldfish pond. Her husband was at work and did not like the idea. In their huge backyard, he could find no room for it.

"The birds will crap in it," he had reminded her when she brought up the idea the night before. "You'll have to get someone else to dig it."

"How deep," she asked, "two feet? I could just stick a plastic wading pool in the hole then."

"No. Three feet, four. At least. I won't clean it either. Don't ask."

"Don't worry, you don't have to clean it. Connie doesn't clean hers. I think two feet would do it. I could dig that."

"Fish will get too big. Then what'll you do in the winter?"

"Bring them inside. Put them in the tank there, that's what it's for."

"No, they'll be too big. I saw some the other day, outside, they had to be a foot long." Mr. Smith held his hands apart, a round Better Cheddar glowing like a coin in each palm.

"No, they'll be fine." Sunny wasn't sure now. Maybe he was right.

"Carp." He shook his head. "I'm not building a pond for carp. Why do you need a pond anyway?"

"Pool. I just want one. How about making it donut-shaped and leaving a center mound of dirt for a birdbath?"

"No. It won't work."

When they'd finished teaching fourth grade that spring, her friend Connie had dug hers shallow and lined it with blue plastic anchored with big rocks along the lip. Then she'd put some water lilies on top and outlined its curves with soft lavender and pastel blue flowers. The image had stuck in Sunny's mind for two months until August, when it seemed to announce itself officially.

"Where're you going to get water lilies?" Mr. Smith shook his head, "I don't know about you sometimes."

Mr. Smith slept on the carpet in the living room that night, the room air conditioner blowing across him and the TV tossing one old movie after another into the inky darkness. She slept upstairs in the heat with a fan sucking the hot night into the bedroom. When Sunny woke up at dawn, they traded places. As she did the bills, she heard the alarm go off in the bedroom. Next he appeared bathed and suited and smiling. His was a magical transformation each workday. When it got hot, she stopped watching him get ready so she could get the effect fresh each morning as he came down the stairs. Magic Man. Clean, handsome, all business. They kissed efficiently like Ozzie and Harriet and she waved him down the street already shimmering with heat.

Where would she get the rocks, she wondered as she paced off the little section of yard in the shade of the cedars and garage. She couldn't remember how wide the plastic was in the garage, but she knew she had a huge, long roll of it, so the pond would have to be coffin-sized. She sort of wanted a triangle that sliced the right corner of the yard, but didn't know whether you had to be able to get all around it. The fence and the trees would get in the way.

By nightfall she'd have the fish out there. "And all the cats in the neighborhood," Mr. Smith's voice intruded from the night before. As she stuck the point of the spade in the ground and shoved on the lip with her foot, she wondered if he were right. Instead of sinking deeply and easily into the ground, the spade struck something an inch down.

Tree roots, of course. She moved back several feet into the hot center of the yard, dry and yellow as a harvested field, and tried again. This time it sank an inch and a half before it stopped. She peeled back a small wedge of grass and soil and looked. It was just too dry. There weren't any roots, but it wasn't going to work anyway. If she turned on the hose to soften it, her neighbors would call the cops. They all watched each other's lawns now for the telltale signs of green.

Sunny stood there, the sun blowing heat onto her earlobes, the point of her nose, her elbows, places she forgot usually, but the drought had become so specific now, having burned the large things, lawns and trees and lakes, it seemed to get personal. The handle of the shovel grew hot in her hands, so she let it drop. The chunk of soil flew up and shattered when it fell back.

Overhead the sky took on the pale, electric blue of a Las Vegas wedding chapel. The grass crackled under her shoes. She felt her legs prickle with heat bumps under her long pants. The air shoved against her like a body, its tongue pushing her teeth apart, trying to reach down her throat.

When Mr. Smith came home, he would tell her how much lower the river had dropped. He would invite her to walk down there and wade across it with him. People had never seen it this low in recorded history, he would tell her. The fish would be gasping for oxygen, dying in the shallows, their big bodies heaving desperately. Sunny and Mr. Smith would climb over them like rocks and Mr. Smith would nudge one with his toe, as if the argument were closed. His shorts would be dirty, and Sunny would notice that he is changing shape, as if all the mass is rising from his feet and falling from his chest, to meet at the equator of his belt.

"What shall we do," she'll ask him.

"Wait," he'll tell her.

How It Got Started

It's stacking up around here, corpses I think I saw on "The Big Picture" late at night when I was growing up. "The World At War," the last thing you'd remember Sunday night as you were falling asleep, and as if the Nazis had never stopped, they kept stacking those bodies relentlessly, with all the patience of Santa under the tree. And it was always the paleness of the flesh, not only the bones that stuck through like tent pegs, but also the whiteness that glowed out of the usual grays of the film—something making the flesh ecstatic as it grew peaceful to its death.

But that's not right, no, because the figures always tense in death—the arms reaching out, the legs drawn up or caught in midair like the deer along the highway in the fall, when the cars can't help but finish their leaps through the air. The deer that are caught with the car, embraced and laid down to rest beside the road, the trail of blood a string bedding the grass and small deer mouth, the legs in eternal motion. With the humans you were always expecting the blood associated with death, but never found it—just hands clawing their way up through air, and mouths open about to say something. The stacking harder because no one fits together, these jigsaw bodies, all angles, the patience of stacking, the flesh probably heavier than it looks, though it seems model-airplane light, and never the darker betrayal from mouths or ears or noses, never hands pierced, or feet or sides, never something to organize this Sunday-night death.

As I watch from my sleep, I want to urge them to iron the bodies, flatten them with the heat of metal, it will be easier to hang them in the closet then. We can wear them in the morning. Mother will want us neat for school. Don't leave them in those stacks to wrinkle and dirty, don't let them get wet out there. It seems in those films that it is always about to rain, or has, but everyone looks dry, as if the water wouldn't come to this part of the world, and it is a dry cool that they live in because no one even sweats. Only the graininess of death impairs the skin. Even the soldiers are living at the proper temperature. No one is more than a figure in a Halloween masquerade, haunting my sleep with pretend ghostliness, wanting a trick-or-treat out of me. Go away, I tell the images, you'll get in trouble if they find you gone from the television. And in a few minutes the other program comes on, the one that they alternate with patience of Nazis—an atomic bomb—and it is never a show we witness as a family. It is never explained. It is always just blowing up, like an inverse tornado I've spent years watching sweep down across the plains.

I've never been able to draw anyone's attention to it. Father is always reading his paper with the impatient clicks of his tongue and teeth. The world makes him mad, everyone is stupid. I don't know enough to agree with him. I think he's just being narrow-minded and want to avoid his attention, get out of the dishes—yes, dinner has been kept for me, it's waiting and gelid on the table. The grease from the meat forms a little skating rink across the plates, and the canned applesauce is a familiar tan, the same room temperature forever on my palate, and a vegetable my mother has cooked faithfully for hours.

She has gone from the table, they have all gone, and there is an atomic bomb on the TV in the living room no one is watching, and I unsling the box of Girl Scout cookies and feel the strangeness of a dinner missed hour. I am out of the routine, and it is as if I stepped in my twelve-year-old life into another house, and something is happening on TV, and the rest are gone, and only the father is sitting there, and he strangely ignores my late entrance. I am uneasy, want it to be explained, but everything suddenly looks different, framed by the explosion as it is, and my falling out of the day like a piece of plastic no one has missed, and I know they haven't missed me and maybe they're stacked in the basement, I think, maybe it all happened and it is all happening. They're televising the atomic bomb and in a minute my father and his chair will go flying up through the roof of the house, his hair standing on end as he tries to hold onto the newspaper disintegrating in his hands. And the others have already taken their positions, stacked, they are ready. Only the dinner, eaten and left for me, is about to fly out of my grasp and I have to go through this on an empty stomach, and somehow that seems sadder than all of it. I want to turn off the end, but the authority of the absent viewer makes me walk by. Wait, wait, I want to say, wait, I have to sell the rest of the cookies and my family doesn't know yet that this is the end.

I go back again to the *Life* magazine photos, to the newspaper headlines of the kind-looking Mrs. Rosenberg, they have so many ways of killing people, I see, it's non-stop, and it's not just television. It is the patience of Nazis. I am frightened by patience the rest of my life, afraid of the ordinary life that surrounds the television nuclear attack, fearful of the mood of the newspaper, of the courts, of the police that take you away and leave your small

children to fend dinner for themselves and put wires on
a woman in a dress who looks like she would babysit me
if my mother would hire one instead of the patience of
my older sister who hates me. And around me, they have
so many ways to kill us.

And late at night, with the taste of Girl Scout cookies
in my mouth—my incredible sales year, when I beat everyone in the troop because I had to accomplish something
before my family realized we had been lost forever that
early spring evening when they televised the bomb,
because I knew that even to record such a thing meant
that they could play it back to us—and yes, late at night
on Sundays when I am kept awake by impending violence
of the week ahead, I drift through Nagasaki and Hiroshima
with the narrator of my wars, assured there is no place
that is not seared, melted, burned beyond recognition.

The bodies black, again no blood (it must be the sign
of the times, I realize, to get around the inconvenience
of blood), modern life, the bodies darkened like house
timbers, charred into shapes that again make them diffi-
cult for the patient workers to handle. Only this time they
use bulldozers, this time the fusion of flesh and household items—a woman holding a bowl, a man in a chair,
a boy and a dog—makes it impossible, and the heavy metal
bucket comes clunking down to break up the eerie sculp-
tures. As I wake for a moment, I notice that no one is angry
with the work, no one impatient with the task. The city
like a building flattened for construction makes it easier
to look around. I cannot imagine it with houses now, and
it looks through these years like so many other places I
see in my sleep, in my walks through other cities, I don't
think I would recognize it. I don't think it looks so different from London in the blitz of Phnom Penh or Hanoi.
I think it looks like a football field littered with the game.
I don't expect that it is more than the empty popcorn
boxes and beer cups. I don't expect that it requires more

than the patience of groundskeepers to sweep up, getting in their little sweeper cars and driving over the grass, sucking debris with a vacuum force. I don't know the stackers, the death that faces us, my family already gone years ago from a nuclear blast they failed to notice. The whole neighborhood living on borrowed time as far as I can see, adjusted to time I stepped out of, forever, that early evening when I chose to sell cookies instead of accept the evening dinner death that was waiting there.

And Mrs. Rosenberg, well, she's looking after the kids, like I always wanted her to, and her husband, a confused but kind father, who used household items in his work—the domestic ineptness of Jello boxes scrawled with atomic bomb secrets. Oh, anyone could watch what I've seen and give the secret away, we know that, but it's too late, of course, that flesh gone white like sugar, something of value, something to feed on when the wind whips around you and your ears feel cold even with the house heat and the late night covers around you. No one is ever cold on television. No one is ever cold. Those bodies naked, stacked in warm death, cartons and cartons of things we buy since that night I came home to find the world had adjusted without me. My father turning the television on like a warning, no one watching, they were all gone ahead, hiding, but I couldn't find them after that night, after I ate the bites of cold meat that sat lumpy and undigested through the week, the tasteless applesauce whose color was its only attribute—have a variety of foods, my mother warned, every meal must have green and yellow and brown, and I can't remember the green except the overcooked mushy beans that she would brighten in her imagination to match the pictures of food in the Sunday sections of the newspapers my father clicked over and she only . . .

But they were all gone, the house uncoupled from reality, from time, like a train car, and I stepped on board for one last look around before they left. I wanted to say goodbye, but no one was there:the neighbors, too—gone, the neighborhood, even the Girl Scout troop, a week later, had that look of patience that left me knowing they had all disappeared on the last train out of here.

I watch television late at night on Sundays to see if I can find them, waiting for them to show up, picking like spectators in the crowd through the ruins for what they can find. They won't recognize me, I'm pretty sure of that. They won't find what they lost when the bomb went off, but maybe they aren't even looking.

My Story

Well, I got this little place over in New Jersey, it was good—just a few friends, hundred people out in the audience, bootleg I imported and a few girls on tap for the fellows who needed that. It was nice. Once in a while I got up and did a little number. I'd learned that kind of dancing—soft and slow around—from my older sister, Nell, and she could do it fine. But she died, got it during the war, influenza, took a lot out of the family. Later Dad with a stroke, Ma just down, never could find out why exactly, just down. The way they talked about a horse or cow up on Uncle Uncle's farm, "she's down now, won't last the night." Then they'd turn away sharp and walk out of the room, letting the news settle in on the listeners like a blanket of dust.

When I think back, it's almost like they were all dead already and the farmhouse empty and dirty, the way it is up there in Deerkill, Pennsylvania, sitting lonely as all get-out, windows busted out from the time the cops came in on us, and animals gnawing away on the wood in winter—not much left. And the kids now, coming up there to drink and make out. Jumping around like wildmen in the lamplight. They keep it low, I know they do. They're afraid of the cops coming back—creeping up the road with their lights turned out, some on foot through the back lot, careful not to stumble over Uncle Uncle's implements thrown all over from that time, twisted and broken. They hadn't need to do that, I told them. "He doesn't know anything about it, leave him alone." But they kept at him, and finally something gave out on him and he went down. The cops got concerned then, realized I was right all along. They just wanted to take it out on someone. "He doesn't know anything," I told them. But he was never the same. Sort of wandered off after a while. We think he must be dead. We're pretty sure of it. Not much to hold him. Esther, his baby sister, my ma, gone, and Edward, my dad—then Nellie. There wasn't much but me after that—I wasn't much.

So the farm sits there. I'm careful about the taxes, arrange through the Courtney boy to have them paid each year out of money they couldn't get their hands on. William Courtney, his father, was my lawyer, and I told him what was what, how I knew I was going to go up this time, but about the money—so there'd be something of us left there in Deerkill. So folks couldn't say that we were driven out or gone to seed, and that's why we lost the place. My family, really my mother's family, settled that land in 1793, and I won't let go of it as long as I'm around, that's for sure. Uncle Rudolph and Uncle Silas, then Uncle Morris (called Uncle Uncle by us kids), they stayed there after the grandparents, then the parents died. Not one of them married, and one by one they dropped, until Uncle Uncle just went off that night.

So it's my responsibility. I take care of it, too. Though I wish I had some way to give it on—some blood to pass it to. It's what there is of us here. Kind of makes me sad when I get to thinking about it. My little place in Jersey's gone, too, but that was different. Jewell was there and I really built it for us. She loved it. Didn't like the farm, the country. Being there confused her: she never knew how to walk, how to move through all that open space. She couldn't find anything to hang onto. Fence lines and trees, it wasn't enough, not the same as small dark corners with tables and soft chairs, booths with curtains that closed up so she could be alone with a person, whispering and laughing. That was Jewell: she needed to shine out of that darkness, that shadow.

The farm was so bright there, or gray, like the last time we went together and Ma and Nell were dead and Pa wandered around like he had a big lump on his head and couldn't stop holding it. Maybe he felt the clot, or maybe he was afraid not to hang onto his eyes. They might drop out. It was November and we had come up for Thanksgiving. Closed the place in Jersey, told people to find their families. We'd all laughed about it, careless, and gone off.

I didn't want to lose anyone else up there, so I had been coming back to Deerkill more regularly for the past few months. But Dad was getting worse anyway. You could tell he didn't think I made up for what had happened to the others. I just wasn't much compensation. Uncle Uncle always had to remind him that I was around. He got so he'd talk about all of us like we were already buried—me included. But I tried to understand, and even when he mixed me up with his brother Orrin, I kept being polite and his son. I understood.

Once, in the corn crib, while I was shoveling out some feed for the hogs, he told me that I had died. I guessed he was thinking of someone else and kept shoveling corn. He was confused a lot. It bothered Jewell more than me. He couldn't take his eyes off her most of the time—watched her moving around the kitchen or hanging out the laundry. It was hard on her, I know. She was used to attention, but the Jersey people were always approving of her.

I guess she went to please me, because her mother, Kate, was still alive down on the Jersey shore. Jewell came up because she wanted to help out, I think. It was a mess, especially after Dad drifted away from his job—dislocated instead of relocated, we used to joke—and came to settle in with Uncle Uncle. Uncle wasn't much better off, though he tried to be neat and clean, and Dad wasn't able to do much of anything for himself.

They lived up there like two old spinsters, and some things got done around the place and other things sort of let go and started to go down. Uncle took care of the animals and they were fine. It was Dad in the house that was the worst. You know, grease spattering around that neither of them had the energy to clean up until we arrived every month or so. And the washing—I know that Uncle tried to get Dad to pay attention, but you know, Ma took care of that for so many many years that he just couldn't get the hang of it that late in life. You could see that kind of idea planted around his lips: they always seemed to bubble out when he was thinking like this, sorry for themselves, real sorry. So those two didn't do much around the house except cook up messes in the kitchen and haul out some trash once in a while. Then toward the end, Uncle Uncle was losing track, too, and the trash that used to be sorted—paper and stuff for burning in the barrel and cans and metal for dumping down the gully along the north field—that stopped, and it all built up right beside the henhouse, then a good wind would come up and blow the papers around, and the chickens would go picking through the garbage and knock the whole pile apart, so that on a windy day you'd hear a constant clicking of cans rolling into each other and broken things rattling around.

Usually, I'd spent most of the visit outside, like I did that Thanksgiving, trying to clean up. I didn't want the neighbors coming up on us like they most likely did when I wasn't around, surveying the place, thinking about what they were going to do when the two old men finally lost out. I had another plan. No one was going to get the farm.

The thing about the place that was nice was the big stand of pine up the mountain. Loggers were always stopping by, wanting to cut some, and occasionally when the family had needed money in the past, it had sold some off, then replanted. The paper mill over in Montrose wanted it all now, but we hung onto it. Then there was a little slate quarry beyond that, toward the top of the mountain— and not a mountain like they have out *here.* These are just huge, dark rocks humped up along the horizon, but those were soft, poured out like honey across the land there, coated with trees but still high enough to make the sun come down and go up later for us. And on a cloudy night, we couldn't see a single light from a single other human being for miles, and you could almost bump into yourself walking around outside. We had good hayfields, too, lots of water from our stream and springs. The cows did fine, the pigs and chickens were good. It was a solid little place.

Maybe the soil was a little too rocky. I was getting after Uncle to do something about the front cornfield. The dirt was getting so washed-out looking and I had done some reading about it. He ignored me mostly, as he did almost everyone. He was such a spare man. Everything he was bespoke economy. He kept planting corn every year in the front field, no matter what, and wouldn't listen when I saw that it was coming in poorer and poorer each time. Not enough nutrients, I'd explain, knowing that the word meant nothing. I wanted him to put in some alfalfa or let me show him how to use some of that new packaged fertilizer, but he wouldn't listen. "Hogs like it," was all he'd say about the corn. "Cows don't care," when I spoke about yield. Maybe he was right, because after they got me out of there a year later, the animals were taken away, and the field never got planted again.

Now I bet the ryegrass and burdock have taken it over completely. And thistle. I swear one day in August I almost had a heat stroke trying to clear the thistle out of the back pasture across from that field so it wouldn't be ruined.

But it didn't do any good. I was out on bail then and came out to see what could be done. I knew, of course, that they'd fix me so I couldn't come back for a long time, if ever. I'm a realist about things most of the time, but it was hard to see the weeds coming up on the place like that. The cows long since taken away, no one ever paid a penny for them either, what with Uncle Uncle gone, me in jail, and Jewell—well, I guess no one even believed we were married, so there wasn't any use in finding what she wanted done.

About noon that day I fetched down the big mowing scythe and took my shirt off and went to work chopping thistle and piling it up—working and cursing off the weeks in jail, the sun burning all hell out of my back and the blisters forming, then breaking, then bleeding on my hands. I didn't care this time, didn't bother to wear gloves—what difference would it make now? I didn't have to take care of myself the same way, wasn't dealing cards or touching Jewell's soft skin like before, so I let the wooden handle buckle up my skin and push into it. Somehow the raw pain felt right. Good. But I only got through half of the weeds before I knew it wasn't going to work. I couldn't stop, though.

I don't know what would have stopped me eventually, I really don't, if old Courtney hadn't driven up with his son. They parked the car half buried in the shoulder-high weeds grown up along the driveway and got out and stood there, watching me for a minute. Then the old man came down the little slope to where I was, his shiny shoes snapping and crunching through the thistle stumps, and called to me.

I knew he was right. I stopped and realized that my hands were a mess because the handle was so sticky with blood. The old man didn't even flinch, just pulled out a white linen handkerchief and told me to wash up in the creek. I almost passed out when I tried to walk, I'll tell you. Then a frog jumping out of my way scared me so that I almost fell dropping back from it. I had spent half my life on that farm trapping those frogs and trying to make them into pets or throwing them into the slop to watch the hogs run squealing around. But it must have been the sun, because even the creek looked strange when I hunkered down, and I was afraid to put my hands in the water, afraid that those shiny pebbles were hiding something just below the surface, or maybe that I would put my hand in where it seemed shallow and never find the bottom—like swimming in a black hole down in the river below us.

"You're dead," my father told me that day in the corn crib. I shoveled the corn. He died.

"Don't ever hurt your uncle," my mother had whispered to me at the end. I was the one who had brought the doctor from the city to see her—"as long as I have the money, what do you care that I spend it this way," I told my father. "She's my mother. She doesn't have to just die like one of Uncle's cows." But she did.

Take care of Uncle. And, oh, I did wish Uncle Uncle lived in that stream, that I could pluck him out of that water like a rock, before the sun dried it dull and ordinary. Oh, I wanted Uncle to come back then, couldn't hardly bring myself to touch that water he might be in.

And Nellie teaching me to dance and dance and dance, and I *had,* oh, I had danced for all my friends down in Jersey. The lights low, with Jewell in the corner shining and my friends drinking and the other girls that worked for me, well, they were doing their jobs, too. But I knew Nell wasn't there. That's why Dad went, and the place got too wild. Oh, I guess it was more Jewell than anything else. That's the truth. She just came home less and less and finally took off week after week, coming back between times to ask me to love her—it just got too hard. So I put Henley in charge of the Jersey place and moved up to the farm to operate things from there. Uncle needed another person around the place, too, I told myself. I was getting it back into shape, I was. Doing the business at night—the trucks bringing the stuff in, storing it in the barn or in the old milk house after I built the new one. That old one, though, had just the right temperature, cooled with those fieldstones that seemed to bring the earth damp with them out of the ground.

Uncle just ignored it all, not acting surprised when he came on two hundred cases of booze tucked back up among the straw in the loft, just working around it. I couldn't tell what he thought, I really couldn't. He was so spare. And I must have been a little crazy that year anyway with Jewell gone, and I was out of the way of talking to anyone else. Uncle Uncle thin as a scythe blade, coming in just at dark to eat what I'd made. He never put on a pound either. And I cooked, oh, I was hungry. Butchered a hog and cured up the meat. Made grape juice once the concords along the garden fence came in and stored it in the fruit cellar, like mother and grandmother used to.

Uncle never gained a pound or a word. He just ate, sopped up gravy pools with his last piece of bread, put his plate on the counter next to the washbasin and went upstairs to bed. Every night. I didn't care.

I didn't have much to say, either. I kept dancing in my head to the music where Jewell stayed so beautiful. I sat by the little lamp that way most nights, waiting for the trucks or cars to come, picking it up or dropping it off. During the day, I put running water into the house and started planning the indoor plumbing. If I kept busy, I could keep going, I told myself that. But I knew it wouldn't last. Anyone could see they were going to follow the operation home sometime. In a way, it surprises me that it kept up for so long. All I did was bury the money, put it in the milk house, to keep it cool and silky as cream. I figured Uncle would need it—I didn't figure on him wandering off. There's always something we forget.

So when the Courtneys came out to get me that day, bring me back to jail because the bail had been revoked, I told them where it was and the old man promised to keep the place going. I believed him, what else could I do? The last thing I remember was looking out the back window, watching all those purple thistle flowers nodding in the breeze, knowing they'd be up in the old cornfield by next year, and I'd be here, where I am today. And with Uncle Uncle gone, my mother would never forgive me.

Working Iron

There's nothing worse than the time in the hall: the cigarette smoke, the hard chairs, the time payments printed on our faces. The thoughtfulness of dirt-packed nails clicking at the plastic armchair arms. The disheveled look of no work. The calculation of bus or gas money, the inevitable beer that waits when the morning is over and no work again. The long afternoon in the bar until the stumble home, the fall into the blister of domestic duty. The kids' faces caged in their rooms, their TV shows. The wife, there's nothing left to say to her. Both of you know the score and can't play the game.

We'd been on our butts through Christmas and most of January when Jack came up the road one Saturday with his ex-wife, his girlfriend and his little girl. We decided to go ice fishing though it was just above zero and the sun breathing like a fist at your eyes. I knew the fish wouldn't be biting. But I stowed the six packs while the ex flirted in a discouraged way, avoiding Jack's eyes. Packed the hacker for the hole, then the poles, the tackle box.

Jack never had anything but women. He wasn't equipped to go anywhere except the job. Took his wire and pliers wherever he went, like he might be called on to wrap a beam, frame concrete. He had brought sandwiches the girlfriend had made. Whole wheat bread, heavy, homemade. Hard to chew. She had jaws like a horse. If she'd put on some makeup, she'd be pretty. Jack didn't want her that way, he told me one day on break when the foreman had to run off and check an accident—some guy stuck in the middle of a tumbling stack of steel. Jack had rescued her from her naval-academy fiancée, from the big expensive wedding, from her money and her future. Brought her up north here, rented that place on the river three miles down the road from me. It had been a store when the mill was standing; now the mill was just a pile of slate shingles and foot-thick beams. We'd get drunk sometimes down at his place and stumble around on the slate pile trying not to fall into the Hudson. It's so swift and broken up, there's a constant hiss I try to stop by putting my foot in to stir up some stillness. It never works.

The girlfriend arrives with her bread spread with something green and brown. She won't let things alone. Everything is chopped and grated and blended. When I eat there, the food is unidentifiable. That's when we drink a lot. And now this.

The ex-wife like a flat tire he's driven the car on because he probably has a flat spare, too. Nothing wire could fix. Duct tape. Big rolls he patches his van with. The kid, though, she's bright as a new bottle. Polite and whiney, both. Can't put my finger on it. Polite to Jack, whiny to the mother, the ex. Must make the mother tired, I decide, and offer her a beer. Something to cheer her up. When it does, I realize that's a mistake, too. On the way over, it's her enthusiasm, like she's invented the day.

I park and climb out of the car, haul the stuff onto the lake just a ways. Find a solid spot. The sun's like a hot hand pushing your head to your boots, and the wind, well, the wind wasn't anything to speak of. Just the icy tongue between the collar and neck. It gets a lot worse up on top, thirty stories on an Albany high rise, and Jack with a spray can painting the kid's name in bright red on a beam, then standing there cool as you please while I snap the picture with this dumb little instamatic he must've had since high school. He takes it back, puts it in his lunch pail. Maybe he never wants a bologna sandwich. Maybe he'd make it peanut butter whether the girlfriend was a vegetarian or not. I've noticed that people who grew up with money could afford luxury like that.

Hacking the hole isn't easy. The ice bites back at my tools. Jack takes a turn. He's built like a linebacker and makes some headway. His daughter is dancing flat little circles around us. The sun's wet light licks the hood of her coat until it glows bright as a blue ball on the back of her head. The ex tries to play with her daughter in that clumsy adult way, like her feet have grown too big for her body. She'd probably dance the same way. I can just imagine her practiced groans in bed, like an animal hit by a car.

While Jack punches holes in the ice for the lines, I pop a couple of beers, lingering with the girlfriend whose tallness would daunt a smaller man. But both Jack and I are tall, both big men, though he's more muscled than me. Her size makes a compliment to us as if she grew for the occasion. If she'd wear some makeup, she'd be pretty, I want to tell her. Instead I smile at her and enjoy the feel of the beer, equalizing the inside and outside.

The ex-wife stands like a witness before the scene of the accident, rocking on her toes, hands shoved in her coat pockets. You can tell when a woman is giving up by the winter coat she wears. The heavy, warm ones are the tip-off. She doesn't think anyone's going to come along and warm her up again. She gets practical. As she stares bleakly at the dark water bubbling up through the hole now, I can tell she isn't really looking for anything anymore.

Jack and I decide that two holes are enough. The women don't care about fishing, and it's only the kid who is still excited. I drop my line in out of habit. The fish won't be biting today.

I sip my beer and jiggle the pole though, watching the pine and fir that surround this corner of the lake, wishing I could tell what the weather'd be like by tonight. Snow. Feels like the cold will hang on. It is now. Won't really give in to the alcohol. I decide that when someone catches something, we'll leave.

The kid is standing next to the hole under the protective eyes of her father. He's made it extra small, so we don't have to worry about some emergency ride home with wet kid clothes. Her head down, the girlfriend is between us two men, but she's not talking to anyone. Everyone is thinking something else. When the first fish comes up, we're packing it in. If not sooner.

Jack wears a spool of wire on his belt—and a measuring tape. The wind ruffles the few hairs that remain on top of his head. He doesn't wear a hat, no matter how cold out it is. On top of a building in winter, I've seen his ears turn so dark you'd think they'd burst. The frost hangs off his beard, his nose, the dark of his ears, those blue eyes drift off like birds set loose as he looks over the city, watching a storm blowing in from the west. The foreman times it so you're not on top when it gets real wet or icy. He pushes to the last minute. Guys go along with it though. We need the money.

Foreman was pissed about the kid's name on the girder. "It doesn't matter," Jack told him, "we cover it up." But the foreman doesn't like him. Told him to take the afternoon off and grow up. It's tough. Child support and wife support and the girlfriend who's used to money working in a hippie natural-food store part-time so she can develop herself. We're out of here five days a week by five A.M., have to drive the hour and a half to Albany—and if the weather's bad, who knows—then back the same at night.

When Jack picks me up, he's already taking the first toke on his pipe. "Just to get rolling," he says, and offers me some. I don't. Don't drink on the job, either. Some guys have to get a start in the morning though, I can understand that. A beer for breakfast, another at lunch. More if the foreman's riding them. I just never got the habit. But then I don't have that discouraged ex-wife you'd have to make payments on like a car totaled out before it was finished being paid off at the bank. And the kid—she's not bad. It just takes more than I have to worry about so much, I decide, and take the last grainy swallow of the bottom of the beer, squeeze the can in half and drop it on the little pile I'm collecting.

It's getting colder, the sun seems to be dropping back a little early, like it got tired and couldn't handle the responsibility. I think about changing the lure, the bait, some frozen smelt, but what the hell—the fish aren't biting today. I know that. I almost told Jack, but I could see that he had to do something with all those women. The trees look like a crowd of people waiting for something. Overhead a sea gull sails without a word out of sight. I miss the hawks in the winter. Like to watch them hunt the valleys and river from the porch. Like to just sit there, safely close to the ground. Sometimes while we're on top, a bird will fly past us and give us a look like we're crazy bastards after all.

The ex has started walking away from us. I don't know about the ice, and I'm about to say something to Jack when the kid starts hollering and jumping around. "I got one, I got one," she says. Oh sure, I think, but she pulls hard and out pops this little fish. It collapses on the ice and lies there, stunned. We all stand there staring at it like

it's a Russian missile or something. Then I pull my line
and start cleaning up.

That's it, I say to them. When I come back from dropping the empties and the tackle box in the trunk of the
car, I see the wife has returned. She's standing with Jack
and their kid, admiring the fish. They won't eat that one,
I decide as the girlfriend moves toward the car and me,
the little bag of terrible food still clutched in her fist.

I go back to make sure we haven't forgotten anything.
Jack is a little careless. He tells me how he loses his bill-
fold all the time. Once made a phone call after cashing
his check, six hundred dollars, and he left it in the phone
booth. I gather them up and herd them before me then,
the excited little kid dancing behind the fish hanging stiff
as a board from the line. I glance at the ex-wife. The coat
says discouraged, but she looks OK without her makeup.
"You caught the only fish," she's saying to the kid.

As we all load into the car, I notice that Jack has forgotten about the girlfriend, so I pull her in after me and
let her thighs press mine during the ride home. It was
going to snow any minute, like I said, and come Monday
we'd be waiting in the Hall again.

Cousin Taber's

Finally we thought we'd go out to Bondsville, where Cousin Taber ran the Lutheran Fishing Camp. We knew they'd been hard hit but were unprepared. First the gas station with the lamp poles waving in the middle of the night like trees after a forest fire. The stumps of pumps in the middle with their heads taken off. Even the little building where you paid, gone. Only the lights flooding the concrete like a mall parking lot. Then the billboards that boxed in every corner. Well, they hadn't been repainted. You could just read the outline of Taber's Lutheran Fishing Camp. The fish that usually leaped up silvery and fat looked like parasites had been at it. You could see it fading into the blue of the water and the blue of the sky.

Then the Bait Store was empty, dark, not the middle-of-the night kind, where the back lighting makes you think of diamonds in the window with the sparkling spooners and lures. You could tell there wasn't anything in the windows of the Bait Store. It was just a cave someone could stick a head into and decide it'd be better to stay out.

"Dan Flankelman, proprietor." Well, he'd be gone. Dan was the one that summer we came up for the second time. Out by the lake, there's hundreds of little spots so we weren't worried about anyone coming up on us. The frogs were as sassy as maitre d's in a fancy hotel restaurant. The bats swooped along the closed windows of the car like tiny black sheriffs patrolling the tamarack swamp we'd parked next to. There was no way to leave the windows open. The mosquitoes would have us in a minute. If I was going to unbutton my blouse to anyone that night, we had to be swimming in our own sweat. That's the only way I like being touched in the summer.

God knows where he is now. The sweet smell of tamarack and pine always brings a shiver and the thread of feel his fingernail made down my front.

The General Store was probably the last to go. It had the courtesy of plywood nailed over the front door. There wasn't any need for the front windows to be covered. This wasn't a place where vandalism happened. You took your anger to the water, ran your boat fast, threw the wife's clothes in, the husband's shotgun. The water gulped it all like it couldn't get enough.

We sat there for a few minutes with the car engine humming quietly. I watched the expert motions of a spider in a web that seemed to gather all the pieces of the town and the night, built across three corners of the door, the store, and the box elder that hung a little dusty over the roof. The spider was herding a moth as big as a rose along her web. Like it was going to appear later in a chorus line, it got dressed and bundled. A care package to her kids. She'd squat and squirt out a silvery spot of eggs. In a few days, the moth would stare impassively at the tiny dots of black that slowly made its body disappear, gradually replacing it with them. I always hoped the moth could only watch, not feel its own disappearing act. Then the wind picked up the web and bounced it like a little silver cradle.

I don't know why we waited there, unless it was to see if anyone would drive through. All around us the buildings sat like boulders. They didn't have any answers. The one brick building in town, the old Hamer house, was always used by whoever was trying to get a business started. But it had failure in the dust or something, because nothing lasted long there. Seeing it empty was nothing new. Tonight it seemed like it had been trying to tell the little town something for a hundred years and had finally succeeded.

The tall hawkweed and ragweed and wild daisies cleaved to that brick like survivors at sea in the little bit of wind sweeping up the street dirt. There wasn't any trash though. Even empty, this was a clean little town.

I think we expected someone to be hanging on. We just didn't know how far it'd gotten. Driving out Highway 6 to our cousin's, we expected more than we got. The bars were gone, blown away, not a speck remained. Like gypsies, they followed the people they could live off of, I guess. Over the little one-car bridge, the hollow bounce of wood planks and gurgle of water like someone pulled the drain of the tub, and starting up the big dark hill. You always expect more in your dreams, I guess.

Then this big, full-sized pickup, jacked up and loaded, starts weaving down the hill at us. It stops and starts, uncertain. The driver's drunk I say silently to my husband. He knows it, though no words are spoken. We put our mental hands of comfort on each other and wait, as the truck stalls above us, sprawling across two lanes like a drunk passed out on a bed. Its headlights shining feebly across the dark at us, weak, like worn-out flashlight batteries. Then he starts up again, taking the hill like it's Mount Everest he's descending, while we wait frozen near the bottom. I look over at the pasture that marks the beginning of Cousin Taber's land, but there's no cows, and in the occasional sweep of moonlight, I can see that the pasture is overgrown, the smell almost overpowering us with its green depth, drowning us in the darkness as we wait the truck out. As it passes us, the driver is drunken even sitting. Weaving angrily on the seat, he waves a can of beer our direction—half greeting, half insult, as he thunders over the little bridge behind us, the boards threatening to buckle under the sudden charge of the huge truck.

As the dust clears, we see the single yard light of Taber's place at the crest of the hill above us. In a moment we're pulling into the farmyard. Cousin Taber himself comes weaving out from between the twin barns, he's looking as overgrown, gone-to-seed as the farmyard itself. And he stares in disbelief at us as we open the doors and climb out. At first he doesn't even seem to recognize us. He's like a dog let out in the country, on its way back to the wild. Then he comes over and uncertainly shakes our hands like it's something new he's just trying out. So this is failure, I think. But it's gone way beyond that, my husband answers silently. We walk through the tangle of weeds to the little fenced yard around the house, open the gate, go up the walk surrounded by huge clover, wild daisies and black-eyed Susans that have taken over from the garden that used to outline the yard. The daisies glow like coins in the yard light and the susans are as dark as animal eyes: come closer come closer, they whisper with a dark rustle.

Inside, Taber's wife is sitting in the dining room at the table with the plastic cloth on it. When she sees us, she starts crying and tries to shuffle her legs under the table, but I see them. "Why, Esther, what's happened to your legs?" I ask. I can't take my eyes off them. She tries to move them again, but the rest of her body doesn't seem to have the strength. Her legs have gotten thin as walking sticks, and they're stuck into these old-lady shoes, but you know it doesn't matter—she can't walk anyway.

At first she just weeps a bit, and I don't touch her. Then she looks up in the dark and says, "We ran out of money—you saw the town. Tomorrow or the next day, we lose the farm. Bank takes it. There's nobody left.''

The next moments are unclear. My husband has been on a winning streak at the tables. He pulls out fifty thousand and gives it to them. So what, I ask him silently. They're confused. How will they live here—her legs past repair? These things none of us say. We just picture the cows back in the fields, their big brown-and-white hides draped like blankets on the backs of chairs, snuffling through the July night heat. And the farm dog, Bully, bounding out to greet us as we drive up. The scent of round, hot, red tomatoes as the knife punctures the skin with a squirt. And the fish lying on the plate, its pink-white meat falling from the careful backbone like a road bisecting the world, the tiny shivers of bone keeping us away.

We all stare out the dining room window. The breeze has died, leaving the tamarack silent in the bottom below.

JONIS AGEE is a native of Omaha, Nebraska, and now lives with her husband, daughter and horse in St. Paul, Minnesota, where she teaches English and creative writing at The College of St. Catherine. Among her previous books are *Houses* and *Two Poems*. *Pretend We've Never Met* is her first collection of stories.